Watch for More Fiction by D. A. MacQuin

from *Indigo Sea Press*

indigoseapress.com

POLITE CONVERSATION ABOUT THE WEATHER

By

D. A. MacQuin

Deep Indigo Books
Published by Indigo Sea Press
Winston-Salem

Deep Indigo Books
Indigo Sea Press
302 Ricks Drive
Winston-Salem, NC 27103

First Deep Indigo Books edition published
December, 2015
Deep Indigo Books, Moon Sailor, and all production design are trademarks of Indigo Sea Press, used under license.

For information regarding bulk purchases of this book, digital purchase and special discounts, please contact the publisher at indigoseapress.com

Cover design by Devin T. Quin
Author Photo by David Pietrandrea

Manufactured in the United States of America
ISBN 978-1-63066-247-9

Special thanks to my family for all their help, and to my husband, Devin T. Quin, for being supportive and creating my cover design.

Contents

Polite Conversation About the Weather,

Part 1   1

Part 2   6

Part 3   16

Patchwork   20

Revelations   37

Across the Ocean   51

Linwood, Illinois   75

A Simple White Dress   91

From Out of Nowhere   101

Woven   124

The Notorious Leah S.   135

Polite Conversation About the Weather

Part 1

After putting on a fresh coat of lip-gloss and brushing her hair, Amy admired herself in the full-length mirror at work. She wore a new white cotton sundress that she sewed herself from one of her mom's old JC Penny's patterns. Her sewing skills improved with each new garment she created. She often received compliments on her dresses, which compelled her to branch out into Capri pants and skirts.

She was irritated when the front door of the diner swung open. *Damn, another customer.* Gathering up her things, she exited the bathroom to take one more order for the day.

"Don't worry Amy—this one's to go," said Bob Peterson, a small, tired-looking man who stood at the counter. She saw the top of his Monroe County Correctional Facility cap, barely visible above the top of the cash register. "I know you folks are closin' soon."

"Oh, hi Mr. Peterson. How's work?" Right away she had a feeling this wasn't a wise question judging from his sad, tired eyes, and weak smile. Last Christmas he told her that he'd worked in the prison for twenty-five years.

"I guess things are about the same...I need a last meal."

These orders always took her by surprise. It gave her the creeps knowing that she was taking an order for the last meal a man would eat in his entire life. She always wondered what the guy did to deserve the death penalty, and if he was actually guilty.

"What can I get for you?" she asked in a small, somber voice.

He pulled a small piece of paper from his breast pocket and read, "Prime rib, medium rare. Mashed potatoes with extra gravy, corn, green beans, a root beer, and a slice of apple pie."

"We're out of apple pie."

"Do you have blueberry?"

"Yep."

"Okay, make it blueberry."

"Is that all?"

"That's it."

She gave the order to Larry, the grill cook, mentioning it was for a last meal. She told him this, hoping he'd take special care preparing it. Orders from the prison didn't come very often. Oftentimes the prison kitchen was capable of providing them. And sometimes death row inmates desired simple things like ice cream, or a salad that Mr. Peterson would get at the grocery store. A few times he went to McDonalds and Pizza Hut to pick up last meals, which he found depressing.

As the prime rib thawed in a microwave, Larry said to Amy, "At least this one's got good taste. Remember the last one?"

"Yeah, that was pretty gross." The last death row meal Mr. Peterson picked up was about six months ago. It consisted of two chilidogs with extra chili on the side, onion rings, fries, a banana split, and a root beer. She thought it seemed like a fantasy meal for a little kid, which reminded her of something she read in a magazine about some death row inmates being slightly retarded.

Amy's boyfriend, Jake, drove up and parked his truck in the parking lot. She recognized the loud skidding of his pick-up truck's tires on the gravel, and his speedy death metal blasting from the windows.

"Larry, I'm taking a break," she said, stepping outside. Jake got out of his truck wearing jeans, hiking boots, and a thick plaid flannel shirt. She loved this look—he reminded her of a big, burly lumberjack. He rushed at her with a wide grin and lifted her up, planting a kiss on her freshly glossed lips. His breath smelled of beer, and his eyes were red and glassy from smoking pot. She didn't like getting high, but it was okay that he did. Pot made her mind feel sluggish, which bothered her because she felt dumb enough as it was. Her secret fear was that he'd break up with her for not being smart enough. Jake looked like a simple country boy, but he was smart as a whip.

She noticed something strange about his eyes. They seemed larger than usual, and a darker shade of blue. "Your eyes look different."

"That's 'cause I'm tripping," he said with satisfaction.

"Tripping?"

"On acid. LSD. You know—*Lucy in the Sky with Diamonds*. The Beatles tripped on this shit all the time. Timmy's friend from Chicago brought it down. Check it out." He removed a small

2

eyedropper vial from his inside coat pocket that was filled with clear liquid. "It's pure. Dealers often throw shit like rat poison and speed in it, but not this." He flashed his ill-gotten gains from Timmy. "You wanna try some?

"I don't know… what'll it do?"

"It's fucking awesome. It makes you super high and energetic. Things start to look and sound weird. And it makes you horny as hell. Nothing's gonna happen to you. I've done it plenty of times and it's never harmed me. Timmy trips all the time and he just got into Harvard. That's why he's havin' a party. Come on—one drop won't kill you."

"How many did you take?"

"Three."

She thought he seemed pretty normal and in control, and he was so excited that she figured one little drop couldn't hurt. If he said it was all right to try it, then it must be okay.

"Come here." He took her hand and led her behind the diner to an isolated place aside massive rows of corn. "Open your mouth," he said.

She did as she was told as he filled the eyedropper and put two drops on her tongue. "How many drops did you give me?"

"Just one. You'll start to feel it in about thirty to forty-five minutes."

They stood quietly for a moment, looking mischievously into each other's eyes. Corn stalks rustled in the wind, and occasionally a car could be heard going by on the never-ending, flat inter-state.

He towered over her, which she loved. He made her feel warm and safe, like her father once did. She couldn't believe how lucky she was to be only sixteen, and already in love with the man she knew she'd marry. Her mother didn't like him. She thought he was too wild and sure of himself.

He gently ran his hand down her cheek as if she were a child. He was proud to be dating the cutest girl in school—so curvy and sweet looking. He prided himself on being able to command her, especially when it came to taking her virginity a year ago. He couldn't wait to exercise his charm around all those delicious preppy girls in Cambridge. He hadn't told Amy yet, but at the end of the school year he planned to go east with Timmy. He felt confident that he'd easily charm people with his rapier wit and dark good looks. He never

3

understood why more people didn't leave town and try to move up in the world. Why would someone like him stay in Linwood? *There's no way I'm gonna stick around this hellhole and work in some fuckin' factory...*

"We just gotta last meal order from the prison. Larry's cookin' it up right now."

"More chili dogs?" he joked with a smile.

"Nope. This one wants prime rib, mashed potatoes and gravy, vegetables, and pie. It's really sad isn't it?"

"What—that they're fryin' some guy?"

"Well, yeah."

"Ha! As far as I'm concerned, it's a garbage disposal. Do you know what that chilidog fuck did? He raped and murdered a nine year-old little girl. How would you feel if you had a daughter and someone did that to her? How would you feel if someone did that to your mom or your sister? Listen—you gotta be real fucked up to get on death row. They're probably fryin' some fuckin' crackhead rapist. And he gets to eat prime rib. Damn..."

She stared at him blankly, not sure how to respond. It always made her nervous whenever he went off on one of his rants. She couldn't tell if he was angry in general, or frustrated with her for not being smart enough.

He noticed the worried look on her face. "Hey—I didn't mean to scare you just now," he said. "I just get mad at the world sometimes. Let's go inside. I gotta take a piss."

"I should probably get back anyway."

They went in through the rear door of the diner, walking past the kitchen where Larry was almost finished grilling up the prime rib. Jake noticed some mashed potatoes and gravy, and vegetables inside a Styrofoam container near the entrance to the kitchen.

"I just need to clean up some tables real quick. Do you want anything to drink?"

"No thanks. I'm just gonna use the bathroom."

He entered a stall and filled the eyedropper almost completely with LSD. Timmy's gonna be pissed, he thought. But he'll get over it. He's rich. He'll get more.

Before leaving the bathroom, he placed his ear against the door, listening for anyone walking by. When he knew it was safe, he slowly opened the door, and walked three paces to the kitchen

4

entrance. He glanced in and saw that Larry was off in the distance with his back to him. In one swift movement, he emptied the entire contents of the eyedropper into the pool of brown gravy contained by fluffy white potatoes.

He went outside towards his truck, got in, and lit up a joint. His heart pounded with the excitement of having committed a secret act of justice. The thought of that rapist-crackhead-murderer squirming in his cell, going out of his mind during his final hours, seemed beautiful to him. *I hate low down trash. Those fuckers shouldn't breed.*

He turned on the radio and a Beatles song was playing. He couldn't remember the title, but it was something from the *White Album*. He began to laugh uncontrollably.

Part 2

Matthew Gold looked at his watch. It was 5 p.m., and fairly quiet for a change. He thought it was pathetic to be happy over such a small detail. Over the past eleven years, he learned to phase out all the noise—the rap music he hated, the fighting, obnoxious banter, and yelling. Thankfully, the Aryan Brotherhood left him alone because of his advanced age, which placed him in the precarious position of being useless. He once joked to himself that Death Row was like high school—he was invisible, except for occasional instances of ridicule. The great irony was that the young, tattooed men with shaved heads didn't realize he was Jewish. His pale white skin was good enough for them. Everyone had to belong to a category. Luckily, he managed to avoid this "mandate" by staying quiet and keeping to himself. He wasn't a threat to anyone, so he survived.

In recent days, he napped more often because he was too angry to be conscious. It was just like the end of his first year when the appeals were unsuccessful, he was broke, and his lawyer was convinced that there was nothing they could do. After coming to terms with the fact that his insanity plea failed, and any legal optimism he once held was gone, he was forced to accept that his wife and daughter would never speak to him or see him again. This wasn't a surprise; Anna told him that this was how it would be. Right after he was convicted and was being led away in handcuffs, she quickly approached and hissed through clenched teeth, "You will never see or hear from me or Leah again." Her eyes were resolute.

There was a lot of commotion in the courtroom, with many cameras and media coverage. It seemed like she couldn't get too close because of the media, or maybe she didn't want to be photographed with him, or maybe she was too disgusted to be near him. Everything moved quickly like flashes of a nightmare; he was too stunned to respond to his wife. Instead, he panicked and looked away, scanning the crowd for a glimpse of his daughter, Leah. He craned his neck around as he was taken away. Leah was easy to spot in a crowd. She was fourteen, but already tall and very blond like her mother. He must have been moving around too much because one of the guards slapped his meaty hand around the back of his neck to steady him. He didn't see Leah. Maybe she wasn't at the trial, or maybe she'd left the courtroom already. These questions were never answered. He was afraid he'd never see his daughter again, and that's exactly what happened.

During his first year, he didn't exactly expect them to visit. Instead, he remained aware that during visiting hours—weekends from 9 a.m. to 3 p.m.—they might appear, or maybe one of them would visit. After the second or third year, (they blurred into each other) he continued to think of them, but not in the context of visiting. At some point, he told himself he wouldn't survive if he continued to harbor hope. Hope felt like punishment.

His relationship with his wife and daughter was reduced to wondering. Leah was twenty-five now and he wondered what sort of young lady she was. Guiltily, he wasn't optimistic considering how much Anna influenced her. At fourteen, Leah already possessed an absolute belief in her own superiority, just like her mother. This was obvious in her carriage and with some of the things she'd say. His daughter's elitism deeply disturbed him, whereas Anna condoned putting down others that she deemed "inferior" or "mongoloid," which for her meant anyone she thought was ugly.

Matthew wondered what other men contemplated before being put to death. He could barely remember what he had for dinner the night before, but he remembered every detail of his life leading up to that night. He saw his life as a string of bad decisions spurred by human weakness. The mistakes were his fault—being an adult entails accepting responsibility. But he couldn't take full responsibility for the motivations behind his mistakes. His underlying reasoning, he felt, was never completely his fault.

For weeks his mind ran a series of "If...then" scenarios. If his parents had raised him to be confident, then maybe he wouldn't have settled for a woman who didn't love him enough. If his mother hadn't gotten sick, maybe he would have moved away. If only...

What if I'd married someone slightly less beautiful and slightly more intellectual? He didn't know any better because he was a naïve twenty-eight year old. For once, his mother was right. *But she didn't like any of my girlfriends, so why would I listen?* His mother grew to be senile and suspicious of all gentiles.

7

Matthew Gold never cared that he was Jewish. He was more like his father—a non-practicing Jew, who claimed to be agnostic. Looking back, Matthew appreciated some of the ethical aspects of Judaism, but he never saw himself as religious. He thought religion was an unnecessary emotional crutch, like having a pet. He saw himself as an individual who didn't have to define himself by race, religion, or any other construct. This had always been his instinct, even as a child. Besides, in the small town he grew up in, no one else was Jewish. There wasn't even a synagogue. Since no one perceived him as being different, then why be different?

He was twenty-seven when he first saw Anna. She worked at a cosmetics counter at the mall where he went to buy perfume for his mother's birthday. He snooped around and made it seem like he was browsing while he spied on her. He checked to see if he was taller than her. They were the same height, so he wondered if this would be a problem. Some girls prefer men that are much larger than them.

If he had met her any sooner in his life, he wouldn't have had the courage to approach her. The timing was right. He made good money as a manager for a real estate agency. He showed large homes to the wealthiest families in the area, which required that he hone his social skills. He liked wearing nice clothes to work and driving a Mercedes (albeit used). His newfound confidence allowed him to approach her.

He should have known something was seriously wrong when after two weeks of dating, Anna Doody made a disparaging remark about Jews. They were in his car at the drive-in theater watching *The China Syndrome*, which starred Michael Douglas and Jane Fonda. She said, "Michael Douglas is really handsome for a Jew." He was caught off guard by her remark so he asked, "What do you mean by that?" She responded, "I thought Jews were dark with hook noses. Aren't their genes all messed up from inbreeding? I thought I heard that somewhere."

"Anna... I'm Jewish."

Her eyes widened as if he'd just sprouted horns. "I didn't know Gold was a Jewish name." He nodded. "I'm sorry, Honey—why didn't you tell me?!" She playfully hit his arm and giggled. "I'm so sorry. Are you mad?"

"No, it's fine. I don't come out and say hey, I'm Jewish because I don't feel like I am. I mean, I was sort of raised Jewish, but I don't follow the religion. I never have."

8

"Oh." He examined her face for any hint of disappointment. It would be cruel to be dismissed for something that wasn't important to him. She looked at him with her sweet smile and said, "By the way, I like your name…Gold."

"You do?"

"Uh huh… It sounds rich." She leaned over and sweetly kissed him on his cheek. "When we get married, I'll be a Golden girl." She giggled at her own joke while fondling him and nibbling on his ear.

His mind raced with a slew of excuses: I'm not religious so it doesn't matter. She wasn't that insulting. She'll change—she's just uneducated. At least she apologized. *It's easy to make excuses when blinded with optimism.*

They married at the Lutheran church, where Anna's family had gone for generations. Both of their families were happy, but puzzled by how quickly it all happened. Her parents were relieved when she told them that they would definitely raise their kids to be Lutheran.

Anna quit her job at the mall and spent her days decorating, shopping, and learning how to cook. Matthew couldn't believe his good luck. His wife turned heads when they were out in public. To him, she embodied what society values in women. She was tall with straight, light blond hair that fell to the middle of her back. She was naturally thin, but still full-figured. Her breasts were plump and her ass was nicely rounded. Her light blue eyes were so piercing that he felt embarrassed to make eye contact on their first date. Sometimes, when they had sex he felt dizzy, as if his head were spinning. Sex with her was unreal, like he was in a dream. Sometimes, he felt guilty that he didn't deserve her.

Matthew looked back on this period of his life as the blind years. For instance, he was glad that his wife didn't have to work, but he should have questioned why she wasn't interested in anything outside the home (with the exception of shopping). When he offered to pay her college tuition, she laughed and said, "Why would I need to go to college when I'm married?"

Anna wanted to have a baby as soon as possible. Sometimes she seemed more interested in having a baby than being with him. He began to wonder if her rush to conceive was "insurance" in her mind that no matter what, she'd be connected to his money. His suspicions about her were muddled and paranoid; he sometimes sensed coldness from her whenever insecurities about her intelligence surfaced. (She accused him of using big words to sound smarter.) But other times, her sweetness and beauty convinced him to extinguish any negative thoughts that could jeopardize their union. He told himself, she's just young and anxious to start our family.

His confusion dissipated when Leah was born. They were thrilled with their baby girl. Anna was a good mother. Matthew found it strange, however, that she overly repeated the comment to her friends and family: "She looks just like me!" It was true—Leah had the same golden glow to her skin, bright blue eyes, and light blond hair. He was glad his daughter would look like Anna. But he heard her express this sentiment enough to wonder if she found him attractive at all. He knew he wasn't the most handsome guy, but he had a certain dark, intellectual look that wasn't common in their small Midwestern town. He was five-foot-eight, with dark brown wavy hair and big, dark brown eyes. He was small, but sharp looking and trim from regular exercise. One of his clients told him he looked like Al Pacino, which made him happy for weeks. He knew he wasn't as striking as his wife, but he always figured women didn't care that much about looks.

Is it six-o-clock already? Two guards opened his cell and told him they were taking him to another cell for his last meal. I know it's my LAST meal, you idiots. They cuffed him and walked him to a cell that looked identical to his usual one. This was where he'd stay for his remaining hours. Bob Peterson, a guard he knew, was on watch duty. He liked Bob because he did his job without seeming to judge anyone.

Matthew sat at the little table in his cell and ate the meal he requested. Mr. Peterson looked up from his newspaper and asked, "Is it all right?"

"It's fine… exactly what I asked for. Thanks, Bob."

"You're welcome."

Bob returned to reading his paper while Matthew's thoughts drifted back to his daughter. She was always so smart… Leah spoke in clear, full sentences by age two, and at three she was reading and constantly asking us to buy her more books. After kindergarten, she skipped the first grade. At the time, Matthew secretly thought to himself, "Thank God she has my brains." There was a silent recognition between him and his wife that their daughter got the best they had to offer—her looks and his intelligence.

Anna's life revolved around Leah. She compensated for everything she didn't have while growing up: a hot breakfast every morning, new and expensive clothes, piano lessons, dance class. Matthew knew Anna was a great mother. But Anna also fostered what he thought of as a "bad seed quality" in their daughter. Leah's awareness of her own superiority could be chilling. Imagine an eleven-year old little girl telling you at dinner, "My miscreant teacher gave me a B+ on my Theodore Roosevelt project. She's just jealous because she'll always be a mediocre school teacher."

When Leah was in junior high, she had a group of girls over for cheerleading practice. She was always the most popular girl. Her friends fluttered around her and agreed with everything she said. I always thought she'd make a great lawyer.

The girls were in the kitchen making sandwiches when Matthew overheard his daughter say, "Thank God that mongoloid Mexican didn't make the squad. Can you imagine?" Everyone giggled, except for her best friend, Hally. She was the sweet one of the bunch, and the one who was destined to be Leah's best friend. The prettiest girls always recognize their equals.

That night, as Anna brushed her hair before going to bed, he asked her if she was aware that their daughter made racist remarks. Anna shrugged it off and said it wasn't a problem. "What do you mean it's not a problem?"

"Let's be honest. All men are not created equal. Leah's a hard worker. If she feels better than others, then she probably is. I thought you said your parents should have raised you to be more confident."

"That has nothing to do with being racist."

"So why don't you say something to her about it?"

He didn't want to say out loud that it was her fault that Leah had racist inclinations. "Mongoloid" was her favorite word for insulting people. That night, he lay awake remembering when he was a little boy and his father first told him about Bergen-Belsen. He wondered how his wife and daughter learned to assume a position of privilege. He always prided himself on being a humble Midwesterner.

He knew Anna was right on one point—he could've been more proactive in disciplining his daughter. But he was afraid. He feared that if he disciplined Leah too harshly, she would stay angry with him for the rest of her life. He knew how she could stay angry for so long. Sometimes when she looked at him, her face lacked any warmth or affection that daughters usually have for their fathers. He pictured her hooded blue eyes in his mind, coolly regarding him as she ate cereal at the kitchen table one morning. She was mad at him because he refused to have an in-ground swimming pool dug in their backyard. He simply couldn't afford it. When she stood up from eating her breakfast, it gave him a little shock to realize for the first time that she stood taller than him. She wore shoes with a little heel that made her stand an inch above him. She strode past him with only a cold, dismissive glance to acknowledge his existence. As he watched her walk down the driveway to school, he realized that his little girl didn't exist anymore. She was now a stranger.

Matthew looked at the clock on the wall. Just a few more hours. He panicked. His heart pounded and he broke out in a cold sweat. It was a half hour after finishing his meal, and now his stomach cramped. He curled up in the fetal position and tried to calm himself with deep breaths. He only wanted time to pass, to lessen the surreal dread of reality, but now he couldn't deny that it was almost time. He covered his face with his hands and sobbed deep, guttural cries. Bob looked up from his paper. He knew to not interfere or say anything stupid.

This was the point where Matthew usually stopped thinking about what he did. But he couldn't right now—the automatic distraction mechanism that usually turned on in his brain was disabled. He experienced thoughts and images that were blocked for years, his TV mind in fast-forward. He couldn't control the speed and flow. He was on his side, staring at the gray concrete wall. Little dark spots and other stains on the wall stood out and glared at him. *Maybe I should talk to Bob. I could make polite conversation about the weather.* For a second he wanted to laugh. Meaningless chatter during the passage to death was absurd. So this is how it goes.

Anna forgot we had theater tickets. This was typical, not that her life was busy. Not that she had a job. It was her idea to see the play. Tom Stoppard. She liked having somewhere to wear her mall dresses. I could tell she was mad. She did that bitchy thing when she holds her head up high, making her neck look longer.

Fucking Danny Sullivan. That fat, disgusting pig. It was after the play, on the drive home. Why did she tell me while I was driving? It's dangerous to drive while mad. Her mind was already made up.

When Leah turned fifteen, we'd divorce. Because then she'd be old enough to handle it. Where did she get this from? Did she read this is one of those fashion magazines? There was no warning. Her head was held high.

They must have been having an affair for a while. His flabby body and fat pig face, with those big nostrils. I could see him huffing and puffing over her like a farm animal. God knows what went through her whore mind. He was rich. That was enough. His big, gaudy McMansion on Brewer Road. People drove past it and said wow, Mr. Sullivan's rich. Leah used to say that.

Does Leah know? Is she upset? I never found out. She might have been happy to move into that big house with the pool. I don't know if she knew about her mom cheating. So much I don't know.

I dropped off Anna and kept driving. My heart pounded and I sweated. I wanted her back, but I knew it was too late. Some things you just know in your gut. I was a stupid fool. I knew something was wrong, but I let myself get suicidal because I was afraid. A lost, sick man carrying around a gun. I'd been carrying around that stupid gun for weeks because it made me feel better. The sickness was back. I had been good for so many years. Nobody had a clue about Wichita years before.

I wanted to believe the problem with Anna would go away. I thought maybe I was imagining things and she would never leave me. I can be neurotic. I can't believe I married a dumb woman. I shouldn't have settled for living here. I was a coward. I used Mom as an excuse to stay. I settled too much.

I saw Hally walking alone on Miller Street. She wore a white sundress and sandals. Hally with the sweet baby face and thin, graceful limbs that future beauties always have. Such long chestnut curls and big brown eyes. She was destined to be Leah's best friend. No one else was beautiful enough. But Hally didn't see herself this way. She was raised to be sweet and humble, unlike Leah. No one ever told Leah to be quiet.

I rolled the window down. Do you need a ride home? Look at you. You're too precious to be walking alone at night. She got in. Why are you out so late? I was walking home from a graduation party because my dad forgot to pick me up, she said. How could he forget you? That's right... Leah mentioned that he was a drunk. She got in the car.

"Was Leah at the party?"

"Uh huh." She looks nervous. Did Leah talk about me? Is she hiding something?

"Did Leah go home yet?" It was almost eleven.

"I... don't know." Anna lost her virginity when she was fourteen. Maybe that's what Leah's doing.

"Was she fooling around with boys at this party? Where was the party?"

"It was at David Gregory's house." You didn't answer my first question.

"Well, was she or wasn't she?"

"I don't know." Her voice was weak and scared. David Gregory... Dr. Gregory's son. Anna told me that Leah's date for the dance was Dr. Gregory's son. I read in a news magazine that junior high kids have sex already, especially in little shit Midwestern towns.

"I guess she's takes after her mother. It runs in her blood."

"M-Mr. Gold. You're driving kinda fast. My street is right h—"

"I know where your street is. I've taken you home a million times. I know I missed it. I just want to talk for a while." My voice was calm. I wasn't scary. I saw her eyes look at the clock. She knows something. She knows if my daughter is fucking already. She knows how Leah feels about me, and about Mr. Sullivan. The thing that gets me is not having a choice. There was no discussion about leaving me. If Leah's having sex already, I'll never find out. She'd tell her mother she lost her virginity and they'd hide it from me. Maybe Dr. Gregory will give her the pill so she can fuck his son.

"Hally?"

"Yes, Mr. Gold?"

"Is my daughter a whore like her mother?"

She began to cry. "Where are we going, Mr. Gold?"

"Answer the question!" I slammed my hand hard against the steering wheel.

She was crying and she struggled to speak. "I don't think we should talk about this, sir." Sir. There she goes with that innocent little polite act. "Please stop the car and let me out!" You're yelling at me? You wouldn't if you knew I had a gun in my coat pocket.

The pounding footsteps of four guards approaching his cell jarred him. Mr. Peterson stood up, and as he unlocked the cell, he made eye contact with Matthew Gold. Mr. Peterson noticed that the mashed potatoes remained on the plate—it was the only food left uneaten. The pool of brown liquid congealed in a bowl of stiff white potatoes. "Actually, I asked for white gravy, not brown," Matthew said. "Maybe I'll have them later." He gave Mr. Peterson a slight, sad smile.

The guards cuffed Mr. Gold and took him to a brightly lit white room where he was made to lay down on a gurney. The doctor covered him from his neck down with a white sheet and tightly strapped him down with several black belts. The doctor then attached to him an EKG and an intravenous line. The buzz of the overhead florescent lights seemed to grow louder.

He wondered if Anna and Leah would see him like this. He separated his soul from them years ago. But at this moment, he wanted them there. As soon as he entered this room, all of his anger and pain disappeared. The story of his life, the analysis of every single detail, all the hurt didn't matter because he was there for one reason—to die for the two crimes he committed. They never found out about the girl in Wichita, but he knew he was dying for her as well.

Any apology—any words uttered about what he did were meaningless. That night with Hally, he let his anger and self-hatred convince him that he was entitled to take something that was taken away from him—a chance to be happy.

A curtain that covered a one-way mirror was drawn back. Through the tears flooding his eyes, he glanced towards the window, but quickly looked away because he was ashamed. He didn't know who was behind the mirror. The superintendent read the death warrant and then asked Mr. Gold, "Do you want to make a final statement?"

He cleared his throat, not sure if his voice would be strong enough to be heard. He took a deep breath and uttered a calm, "No."

The first of three chemicals was injected into him. His mind went directly to a place he hadn't been in years. It was a perfect sunny day at the park. They were having a picnic. He watched Anna fly a kite and hand the string to Leah, who was two years old. Leah gazed up at the sky with a look of pure wonderment. She let go of the string and squealed in delight as she watched it float higher and higher.

Matthew Gold said nothing because he wanted to give his family, Hally's, and the other girl's family, a good death.

Part 3

In the woods outside of Timmy's house, Amy sat on the ground with her knees pulled in to her chest. She leaned against a tree, and stared blankly into the wooded darkness. The din of the party continued in the distance. "Come on, Baby," Jake pleaded. "You didn't think I'd stay around here did you?" He stood above her, impatient to get back to Timmy.

Tears fell steadily down her cheeks as her dreams crumbled. She thought it was cruel that he'd give her LSD and break up with her. Did he plan this? She wanted to tell him this, but she knew her words would come out jumbled. Her mind echoed with all the things he said that made her think they'd be together forever. Tremendous sorrow sat at the pit of her stomach as a wave of nausea rose and fell.

Jake felt bad. Her crying and silence made him feel guilty for getting her so high. He noticed she was sitting on the damp ground getting her new white dress all dirty, which she normally wouldn't do. He felt sorry for her—she cared so much about her clothes, which indicated to him that there wasn't much else going on in her head.

He glanced around and told himself that she was safe. No one would notice if she sat here by herself for a while. "Well, obviously you're in no condition to talk about this right now," he said. In a gentle voice he added, "Look, Timmy and I are going to Hardees for a little while. Do you want anything?" She didn't respond. "We won't be gone long, okay? We'll talk when I get back." As he quickly walked away, she lay down on the damp ground and looked up at the sky.

Timmy's friend, Henry Bright, had been watching them the whole time. He was the only other person who noticed that Amy was crying. They'd been in the same class since the first grade, and he liked that she was one of the prettiest girls, but also managed to be nice. It annoyed Henry when aggressive upper classmen scooped up the cute girls in his class like vultures. He got along with Jake all right, since he and Timmy were on the debate team, and Jake went to their tournaments to watch and support everyone. Henry had to admit that he liked it when Jake called him "a total badass" after a tournament when he made strong arguments against gun control. But Henry didn't like Jake, whom he thought was way too impressed with himself. Even though Henry looked up to Timmy as a cool senior who proved that you could be both nerdy and popular, he thought Timmy was morally weak for conforming to Jake's drug use.

At two in the morning, Hardees was the only place open in town. Jake and Timmy made their way through the parking lot giggling like giddy little boys. They were "peaking"; their acid trips had altered all of their senses and heightened their euphoric emotions. Jake felt lucky that he didn't wreck his truck on the way there considering every traffic signal created traces of light that trailed in his peripheral vision. He felt confident that even under the influence of a hard drug, he could stay in control.

The boys had been best friends since they were eight-years-old, and tonight was a momentous occasion to celebrate. For years they talked about moving away together, and now it was happening. They felt sorry for their classmates who would try to sustain their popular smugness at the local college. Some of them would work in a factory, or the prison, impressed by making ten dollars an hour. Boston was a different planet as far as they were concerned.

The bright lights of the fast food restaurant interior, coupled with elevator music made for a surreal environment under the influence of LSD. Altogether it was a strange and unusual day considering Jake had put the drug in a death row prisoner's last meal, (which Timmy found hilarious), he broke up with Amy, and Timmy bought their plane tickets for Boston. Earlier, Timmy commented that he felt like they were in a movie, and had no idea how it would end.

Adding to this strangeness was the sight of two tall, gorgeous women ordering food at the register. One of them was blond, and the other had long black hair. Timmy thought the blond was the perfect woman—exactly the type he'd want to marry one day. She reminded him of Grace Kelly with her white-blond hair pulled back to reveal a gentle, angelic face with light blue eyes and creamy smooth skin. Both of them were dressed casually, yet still looked stylish and sexy. Women like this didn't exist in their town. The boys gave each other a surprised look as they approached the register. As they ordered milkshakes and hamburgers, the women sat down together in a booth.

17

"They must be from out of town," Jake murmured with a stoned, sly smile on his face.

"Should we talk to them?" Timmy asked. He often relied on Jake for advice with women. His high I.Q. did not guarantee erotic success.

"Sure. Just try to be calm." Timmy's small, wiry frame sometimes made him react to drugs with hyperactivity. And his extreme shyness made him awkward.

They paid for their food and walked over to the women carrying their trays. Jake said in his regular cocky voice, "You ladies aren't from around here, are you?"

They looked at him blankly and replied in unison, "No." The blond one added, "We're just visiting."

"Oh." Jake nodded his head. "By the way, I'm Jake, and this is my friend, Timmy."

"I'm Leah, and this is my friend, Estrelle." The dark-haired woman flashed a bored smile.

"Where are you two from?" Jake asked.

"We're visiting from New York," said Leah.

"Are you both models?" Timmy blurted out, barely removing the straw from his mouth. Jake flashed him the "watch yourself" look.

The women smiled and laughed a little. "Actually we are," said Estrelle.

"That's really interesting," said Jake. "It's funny that you should mention New York because Timmy and I are celebrating our big move to the East Coast in a few months."

"Where are you moving?" Leah asked.

"Boston. Timmy got accepted into Harvard."

"That's really great," said Leah. They both conjured a warm smile for Timmy, making him feel like his future was going to be grand.

"Mind if we sit down?" Jake asked.

The women looked at each other and shrugged indifferently. "Sure," said Leah, appreciating the distraction. They were used to young men eagerly wanting to be near them, and they were too tired to care.

"What are you two doing here?" Jake asked. Estrelle glanced at Leah, whose gaze focused downward. Neither of them said anything. "I'm sorry. I didn't mean to be nosy. It's just that we don't often see

New York City models here in Linwood." He laughed nervously to ease the tension.

Estrelle ate her salad as Leah folded her hands on the table and looked Jake in the eye with a slight smile. Her flawless face was calm, and her light blue eyes were piercing, making both boys uncomfortable. In a flat tone she said, "I came here to witness the execution of a man who raped and murdered my best friend when I was fourteen."

The prison, Jake thought. He gave Timmy a shocked look, which left them both stunned, especially in their drug-induced state.

"I'm sorry to hear that," Jake quietly said.

"It's okay really. It happened ten years ago."

"What was his last meal?" Timmy asked, thinking about the mashed potatoes and gravy. Jake kicked him under the table and glared. Why would she know what his last meal was?

Leah stared at Timmy with barely concealed disgust. She responded to him with measured coldness, "Let's see… I'm pretty sure he had spaghetti with meatballs, corn on the cob, a grilled cheese sandwich, lasagna, twelve apples, twenty-seven pies, a tuna fish sandwich, mashed potatoes and gravy, a liter of ginger ale…"

Timmy began to weep. His body shuddered as he covered his face with his hands. Leah quit speaking and everyone looked down. Jake wasn't angry with his friend; he just felt bad. He reached for a napkin so Timmy could wipe his tears.

Leah felt guilty. He didn't mean to be rude, she thought. These are just young boys who don't know anything. And they're clearly fucked up. Both women recognized that the boys' glassy red eyes, big pupils, and hyper manner at two in the morning meant they were on something. They of all people would know.

Suddenly Leah realized that she felt worse for Timmy than she ever did for her own dad.

Patchwork

It was nearly three o'clock, and Henry Bright hadn't sold one quilt. He sat at his booth that displayed his handiwork—quilts of various sizes, colors, and designs. He was hot, and he once again slipped into one of his dark moods. He began to wonder if his therapist's recommendation of finding a hobby was just plain bullshit. A year ago, he told Henry that cultivating a hobby was a great way to calm the mind, and maybe meet new friends. Quilting didn't result in any friendships, but his new hobby had been good to him over the past year. He liked feeling that he was good at something, and he looked forward to selling his work at the Linwood Arts and Crafts Fair. He viewed his quilts as veering more towards the arts, as opposed to the crafts.

The other booths at the Fair were set up in the parking lot adjoining the courthouse and the bank. Surrounding him were hand crafted jewelry, bird feeders, God's eyes, knitted afghans, and other regional largess for sale. The annual fair was part of Linwood's five-day Peach Festival. There were rides, a parade, and the highlight of the celebration— a beauty pageant that crowned the new Ms. Peach Festival, launching the winner to compete for the title of Ms. Illinois.

Henry was mortified when he learned that his booth would be situated next to Pete Dugan's. He'd known Pete since they were in the fifth grade. He was one of those guys who always had his classes in the "LD wing"—the section of school where learning disabled classes took place. Pete was mildly retarded, but not in an obvious way, making him all the more disturbing.

The Peach Festival was Pete's passion. He spent the months leading up to it constructing his own float for the parade, consistent with the Festival's theme. And he always sold wooden ducks at the Arts and Crafts Fair, which he carved and painted, sometimes in outlandish, metallic paint that he'd steal from the EZ-Mart.

Henry did his best to avoid Pete's attempts at conversation; it was an annoying throwback to high school when Pete would sit down next to him in the cafeteria at lunch. Henry wondered why the mildly retarded and socially inept tended to feel comfortable around him.

"Hey Henry," said Pete, grinning widely.

"What do you want?"

"You wanna see my best ducky?"

"No."

Aside from Pete and a few grandmothers who visited Henry's quilt booth, he didn't garner much interest in the public. Bitterness brewed, especially when he noticed that Mrs. Ivey's quilt booth was immensely more popular. Of course they're going to go for that boring, traditional quilting style of block patterns and conventional colors, he thought. How could I expect them to understand subtlety? Amateurs.

Just as he was considering packing up and leaving for the day, he noticed a small, strange girl browsing through the stalls. She wore a flowery summer dress with thick, clunky black leather shoes, and a large straw hat that looked too wide for her small frame. She came to Henry's booth and stared at his prized possession that hung on display behind him. It was his largest quilt, made for a king-sized bed. She hovered closer and continued to ogle it, as she intermittently sipped her lemon shake-up and chewed on the straw.

In a small voice she asked, "Are these your quilts?"

"Hand-made."

"You quilted them?"

"Yep, all of them."

"That's really cool. I never heard of a guy quilting before."

"Thanks." Henry could tell she wasn't from Linwood. Most girls from around there didn't engage him in such a friendly, easy-going manner. In Linwood, his social status had been ascertained by the time he was eleven, as if it were branded on his forehead. He wasn't outgoing, athletic, or handsome. In high school, he was a talented debater, but that wasn't enough to impress anyone. He likened his existence to being a benign backdrop for the town, no different from the Dairy Queen on Main Street, or the omnipresent cornfields.

She said to him with a shy smile, "You're gonna think this is a strange question but...is that quilt about, *Dune*? You know, that science fiction book?"

His heart skipped a beat. The hours spent sitting in the humid, ninety-degree heat while being ignored culminated to this one

21

instant. He didn't care that no one bought his quilts. He was satisfied that at this moment, at least one person— a cute girl no less— recognized his artistic efforts.

"Yes," he replied. "It *is* based on *Dune*. Wow. I can't believe you recognized it."

"Yeah, well, I read the book, and I recognized the sandworm, the Fremen people, and Paul Atreides with his glowing blue eyes. And right over there," she said, pointing at the top left corner, "that's the Baron Harkonnen floating in the air, with Alia underneath him. That's the part where she's about to kill him, right?"

"You're totally right." he replied. "Wow."

"Do you have any *Dune* stuff for a twin size bed?"

"No, not for a twin. But I have this." He laid out one of his favorites. It was a twin-sized quilt consisting of images from a science fiction novel titled *VALIS*. It was written by his favorite writer, Philip K. Dick, and it depicts a man who comes into contact with what he calls a vast, active, living, intelligence system. This occurs when a young woman from a pharmacy comes to his door to deliver his medicine. She wears a fish necklace that suddenly emits a luminescent pink light, which gives him the ability to see the past and future at the same time, and also speak another language. He depicted the light by sewing various shades of pink material in a sunray-like pattern.

"So you're a PKD fan too. This is totally awesome," she said.

"You've read *VALIS*?"

"It's one of my favorites. I'll take this one. It would make a great souvenir to remind me of this place."

"I figured you weren't from around here. Where are you from?"

"I'm from Dale." She blushed and looked down. In a quiet voice she continued, "I'm... um, h-here for the pageant."

"I'm sorry, I didn't hear you?"

"I'm here for the M-mmiss Peach Festival Pageant. I'm c-competing."

"Cool...that's really great." He thought she was adorable, but maybe a little too short and a bit heavy to compete against all those tall, leggy girls. But he didn't like that lanky, standardized form of beauty. He found most conventionally attractive people to be boring.

His genuine enthusiasm seemed to comfort her. She shrugged and added, "I don't expect to win or nothin'. My Dad thought it would be good for my confidence."

How odd, he thought. Beauty pageants struck him as instigators of eating disorders and shame. "I'm sure you'll do fine," he said.

She smiled sweetly, but conveyed in her countenance that she didn't really believe him. "So, how much is the quilt?"

"It's eighty dollars."

"That's a good deal. My gramma used to quilt. I know how much time and effort goes into these things." She reached into her purse and handed him the money.

"Thank you so much! By the way, what's your name?" he asked.

"I'm Maybelline."

"I'm Henry Bright." He stood to shake her hand and realized how petite she was, which he found incredibly attractive. He wanted to walk next to her and protect her from anything she needed protection from. He meticulously folded her quilt and put it in one of the many Piggly Wiggly grocery bags he'd saved. He took his time with the task; he wanted to talk with her more, and maybe ask her out. But he didn't know what to say, or what they'd do. Linwood was a small, boring town. There was always the movie theater, but it was run down, and it was Friday night, which meant that it would be populated by loud, junior high kids. Or maybe he wouldn't ask her out at all. In the past he'd been accused of being overly anxious with women. He could already imagine the off-putting expression that would form on her face after being asked out.

Interrupting his thoughts, she asked him, "Would you like to come to the pageant tonight?"

"I would love to come to the pageant. Maybe afterwards we could grab a bite to eat or something?"

"That sounds great. I can leave your name at the door so you'll get in for free."

"Okay."

"Well, I should probably go and get ready. I am so nervous. I'll see you later!"

"Yeah, see you at the pageant!"

He watched her walk away with the quilt, feeling like a fool for not offering her a discount.

Like any native of Linwood, Henry possessed fond childhood memories of the Peach Festival. For him these centered around sneaking into the pageant with his friends to gawk at the swimsuit competition. They'd ride their bikes to the high school, where the pageant took place, then listen at the door of the auditorium for the swimsuit competition to begin, which was usually after the fifteen-minute intermission. They would then slip through the doors, knowing that even if they were caught, it would be unlikely for anyone to make a fuss over them in the midst of the pageant.

The open display of supple, womanly flesh boggled Henry's young mind. He viewed the beauty contest as an almost bacchanalian celebration of pure, sexual energy, although he wasn't capable of articulating this idea at the time. The fact that the mayor, and many of the affluent Linwood families attended the event always struck him as odd; gawking at beauties seemed unlikely in the confines of a high school auditorium.

The girls would be lined up wearing swimsuits and high heels—a contradictory fashion combination. Who swam wearing shoes? Their nervous smiles, complimented with big, stiff hair, and heavy make-up, transformed their young faces into maniacal masks of fierce competition. Each girl aimed to outshine everyone else, and bask in the glory of validating her attractiveness. Victory entailed being enshrined in the town's history. The winner would cherish her trophy and tiara for the rest of her life. Her family photo album would insure that one day her grandchildren would be able to proudly boast, "My nanny was the Peach Festival Queen!"

The high school teachers, the school Principal, the families and boyfriends of the girls—they all sat in the audience convinced that the beauty contest was as normal and American as apple pie. Henry saw the presentation as a sexual auction of sorts. He never understood why anyone viewed it as anything other than this. The girls walked down the runway, emoting personal pride as prime specimens of femininity. As they returned to their place in line, you could see the exact shapes of their asses, their firm, taut thighs, and strong calves. Bliss...

When the night was over, Henry would then go home and masturbate, dwelling on two or three of the beauty contestants, and imagine alternative forms of competition that could take place on the brightly lit stage.

Henry felt anxious for several minutes after Maybelline left his booth. She seemed sweet and innocent, not at all like the type to parade her flesh before a crowd of strangers. He wasn't sure if the nervousness at the pit of his stomach was for her, or for himself. Pete seemed nervous as well as he stared, dumbfounded, at Henry with his mouth agape. He held a purple and gold duck to his breast as if he were cradling a baby.

Henry almost never went out on dates. And whenever he did, he was acutely aware of the unspoken mandate to act as normal as possible, although he wasn't sure of what "normal" behavior was. All he knew was that for as long as he could remember, his experience with women resulted in them finding something distasteful about him—something beyond his recognition. He suspected his looks weren't the problem. He was a normal looking guy. Tall and thin, which he considered advantageous, hair the color of dark chocolate, and hazel eyes. On a few occasions, girls from the nearby university asked him out, singling him out for his dark, brooding looks, but polite bearing. Whenever girls would break up with him, he wanted to ask, "What is it exactly that compelled you to dismiss me?" But he never asked. He figured he wouldn't get an honest answer.

Over the years, he grew accustomed to rejection, so he made efforts to see himself as a tortured artist instead of just tortured in general. He took drawing classes at the university, which unveiled a competent, but mediocre talent. It wasn't until he took up quilting that he began to feel satisfied artistically. It distracted him from nagging self-consciousness, and convinced him that rural environments breed artistic eccentricity.

It felt strange entering the high school. He hadn't been there since he graduated twelve years ago. He could've gone to his ten year reunion, but opted not to because he didn't see the point. Having lost touch with the few friends he had, he found high school to be an unpleasant social experience where he strove unsuccessfully to fit in, except when it came to the debate team. Most of his classmates were now married with kids, and would probably think he was a weirdo, or perhaps homosexual since he was still single.

He got his ticket and sat as close to the stage as possible to get a good view. He found it funny that after those years of sneaking into the swimsuit competition, here he was—a guest of one of the contestants. He wondered what they could do after the pageant was over. It would be late, and the only restaurant that would be open

25

would be the twenty-four hour Denny's in Bristol, the next town over. It would be a twenty-five minute drive, but this would give them a chance to get to know each other. Then maybe they'd take a drive through the State Park and walk around the lake. The stars would be out and it might be romantic. Suddenly, he felt that nervous feeling at the pit of his stomach again. He wondered why she even asked him out. Was there something wrong with her?

Henry noticed that sitting two seats over from him was Principal Lee. Henry ignored him. He couldn't stand the guy because he represented that contingent of people from Linwood who considered themselves higher class. Henry remembered that Mr. Lee catered to the popular kids—the football and basketball players, the cheerleaders, and the sons and daughters of the affluent. People like Mr. Lee contributed to high school being an unpleasant experience.

Henry looked at the stage to avoid making eye contact with anyone else he might know from high school. He did this for the same reason why he didn't go to his reunion. On a certain level he was embarrassed by not having a career, like most people his age. When the reunion took place two years ago, he was employed at a video store. And currently he didn't have a job. Instead he lived off the money he inherited from his family. He hated how people equated what you do with who you are.

He was relieved when the lights dimmed and the high school band played *The Star Spangled Banner*. Everyone stood and faced the flag, which waved due to a small fan mounted on the wall that blew air on it from an angle. Mr. Klein, the emcee for the evening, then took the stage to announce the beginning of the 1996 Ms. Peach Festival Pageant. Mr. Klein was the high school librarian, and had emceed the pageant since Henry was a little boy.

The band played Stevie Wonder's *Isn't She Lovely* as the girls entered the stage wearing evening gowns. Each one walked up to the microphone to introduce her name and which town in Illinois she was from. "Hi, my name's Kelly Reed and I'm from Rantoul!" "Hello, I'm Casey Meyer and I'm here to represent Blue Bud!"

When Maybelline took the stage, her smile looked strained, and she didn't stride as gracefully as some of the others, as if she weren't used to walking in high heels. "Hi, my name's Maybelline Carter, and I'm from… I'm f-from D-dale." Her slight stutter was apparent, but barely obvious considering she didn't speak very loud into the microphone anyway.

"Ladies and gentlemen," said Mr. Klein, "here they are! Take a good look at these ten lovely ladies because one of them is going to be your new Peach Festival Queen!"

The crowd applauded and cameras flashed at the spectacle of women in shiny gowns and big hair, all lined up with huge smiles on their faces. Henry could easily see the disappointment on Maybelline's face, even though she attempted to feign happiness like everyone else. Henry sensed that she knew how out of place she was. Her dress was decorated with sequined flowers, while all the others girls wore solid colors. She was the shortest girl, and her hair and makeup didn't project that she knew how to style herself for the stage. It was clear that she didn't have any pageant experience, like some of these girls who have vied for years to win a local pageant so that they could compete for Ms. Illinois and eventually Ms. America.

After the girls exited the stage, Mr. Klein intoned, "Our first competition for the evening will be the talent contest."

The first girl to take the stage was a tall Barbie Doll blond dressed in a mint green, regal gown with long sleeves and silver trim that captured the light. She sat demurely behind the grand piano on the stage. Placing her hands on the keys, she shot one more cutesy smile at the judges. Jeez, Henry thought. She's probably going to play something stupid.

When the crowd was sufficiently anxious for her to begin, she filled the auditorium with a piece from Debussy's *Suite bergamasque*. Henry instantly recognized the piece because he had it on LP at home. It was one of his favorites that he often listened to while quilting. He was shocked by how perfectly she played the piece. It began with a delicate bass clef introduction. Then the melody comes in, plucky and staccato, with the perfect dose of smoothness in the right parts. Her hands moved in perfect synch, with an excellent sense of expression—especially in the parts where there are two separate time signatures in the bass and treble clef. When she finished, the crowd was generous with applause. Henry was stunned.

The next four girls to take the stage paled in comparison. Henry actually felt embarrassed for one of them who delivered a cheesy speech about the pride she feels when she looks at the American flag. He hoped that he wouldn't feel the same with Maybelline.

When she finally entered the stage, Henry was surprised to see her in a majorette's uniform, carrying a baton. He wasn't yet prepared to see her baring flesh. Her uniform was shaped like a one-piece swimsuit, worn with white sneakers. The uniform was white, and decorated with red and blue sequins. He thought she looked very attractive. Her mid-section was a little heavy, but her legs were shapely and muscular.

A recording of Duran Duran's *The Reflex* came on, and she began her routine. She twirled with confident fluidity, as if she were truly in her element. Her smile was genuine and natural—clearly she was an experienced majorette. The crowd seemed to enjoy her routine, which wasn't surprising considering baton twirling was a staple in American beauty pageants. There was scattered applause during an especially high toss of the baton into the air while she spun around several times.

She moved closer to the judges, as if she were trying to project herself more directly towards them. Then, disaster struck. She tossed the baton high into the air again, and it landed off the stage, almost striking a judge on the head. A disappointed "Aw…" swept through the audience. Maybelline stood facing the audience trying to quell a panicked expression as she waited for a woman in the front row to hand it back up to her. As she attempted to continue with her routine, the song ended. The crowd applauded lightly as she took a bow and left the stage with a look of failure on her face.

Henry felt bad for her. All he could think of were things to say to make her feel better such as, "You looked really great!" and "At least you completed most of your routine."

After the rest of the girls competed, Mr. Klein announced that there would be a fifteen minute intermission and reception in the cafeteria.

Henry made his way to the cafeteria and anxiously scanned the room for Maybelline as the contestants appeared in their evening gowns to mingle with the crowd. He spotted her sipping punch and anxiously looking around the room. "Hey!" he said with a smile.

"Henry," she said, clearly relieved. "I'm glad you made it."

"Are you kidding? I'm happy to be here."

"Henry—" She beckoned for his ear and raised up on her toes. "Let's get outta here."

"What do you mean?"

"I'm not finishing the pageant. There's no way. I want to pack up my things and leave now."

"Wait—don't you have any family or friends here in the audience?"

"No." Her eyes began to look glassy. "There's no one here."

"Oh." He found that odd. He assumed one or both of her parents would be in the crowd. "Are you sure you want to leave?"

"I'm absolutely sure. Will you meet me out front?"

He nodded. "I'll pull the car up and meet you outside."

"Thanks, Henry." As she hurried off to get her things, he noticed that she had her sneakers on under her gown.

By the time he pulled up in his orange Volvo, she was waiting in front of the high school wearing a t-shirt and jeans. She carried a garment bag and a big duffel bag. When he unlocked the door, she hastily threw everything in the backseat and got in.

"Is everything all right?" he asked.

"Everything's fine now that I'm out of that nightmare."

"I'm sorry you dropped your baton."

"It wasn't just that. I also stuttered during my introduction. I couldn't help it. I was so nervous." Her brow was wrinkled.

"Don't worry, it wasn't noticeable. I probably would've done the same."

"And how could anyone compete with that classical pianist?"

"Well, I guess she was pretty good."

"Hey—I really appreciate you taking me away from all that."

He was glad to see her finally smile. "It's my honor. So, where are we going?"

"Would you mind taking me home first? I'd love to scrub all this make-up off my face. I feel like a clown."

It was a short drive to Dale, which was a small farm town like Linwood, but even more isolated and nondescript. She directed him through the main drag in town further out into the country, where there were houses and farms situated off of a winding gravel road. "I live out in the boonies," she said.

"It's peaceful out here."

"I should warn you. My dad might be home. He's kinda weird."

"Weird like how?"

She shrugged. "I don't know... I guess he can be kinda crusty.

29

But don't worry. He's harmless. It's right over here." She pointed to a driveway that led to a small, dirty white-shingled house. Automotive parts and empty beer bottles littered the front porch.

They entered the house to a loud living room blaring an action movie on a big screen TV that was much too large for the room. She set her keys down on the kitchen counter and then peered into the fridge, as if by habit. "Dad? Are you home?" she yelled.

A burly man appeared in the kitchen wearing jeans and a flannel. "Jesus. You scared the shit out of me. What are you doing home so early?"

"I left the pageant early."

"You mean you just walked out in the middle of it?"

She nodded silently.

"After all the time and effort you put into this thing?" His face was flushed with anger, making Henry uncomfortable, partly because her dad hadn't acknowledged his presence yet.

"Uh, Dad... th-this is my new boyfriend, Henry Bright."

"Nice to meet you." Henry held out his hand. It took him a moment to process that she just referred to him as a "boyfriend." This was unprecedented, and he wasn't dissatisfied.

"You can call me Frank," he replied. He shook Henry's hand, regarding him suspiciously.

"We'll be in my room," Maybelline said as she grabbed Henry's wrist and led him down the hallway.

"We're not done discussing this, Maybelline."

Her bedroom had pink wallpaper and carpeting, with white, girlish furniture. On the walls and shelves were remnants of past happiness: baton-twirling trophies, a blue ribbon from a track and field event, a prom photo of her in mid-blink, standing next to a red-haired Ichabod Crane. He perused her book collection that included Frank Herbert, Philip K. Dick, Heinlein, Gibson, and Asimov. He was flattered to see the quilt he made covering her bed, despite its odd aesthetic juxtaposition.

She flopped down on her bed and covered her face with her hands. "He's pissed."

"He didn't seem that bad."

"No. He's totally disappointed in me."

"Why didn't he go to the pageant to support you?"

"I don't know. He said he would."

"Why didn't you ask him why he wasn't there?"

"I don't know. I guess I don't like asking him questions."

He wanted to ask her if he was really her new boyfriend, but clearly she was preoccupied with other matters. Besides, he figured it was too soon to discuss their relationship.

Frank pounded on the door, startling them. She sat up quickly. "Come in."

He flung the door open. "I just got off the phone with your Aunt Debbie!" There was a pause while Maybelline and Henry wondered what this conversation with Aunt Debbie entailed. "She drove all the way from Cape Girardeau to see you in the pageant and she said you just disappeared at the intermission without talking to her. She asked the pageant coordinator what happened to you, and she found out no one knew what in the hell happened to you!"

"I d-didn't know Aunt Debbie was coming. Why didn't she tell me?"

"I don't know why she didn't tell you. That's not the point. The point is, I wanna know what the hell is wrong with you? I thought you said things were going to be different now. I spent almost a hunnerd dollars on that dress for you!"

"Dad?"

"What?"

"Why didn't you come to the pageant tonight?"

"No," he said shaking his head, "Nuh uh. This ain't about me. This is about you. Girl, you gotta learn responsibility. When you start something, you gotta finish it! That's what you have to do to make your way in the world." He slammed the door shut. A moment later he re-opened the door and said, "Henry, I'm sorry you have to witness all this. But she's gotta think about what her problem is!" He shut the door.

Maybelline curled up into the fetal position on her bed, hugging an old, beloved brown teddy bear. She began to cry. Through her tears she said, "I don't know what's wrong with me."

"There's nothing wrong with you." He sat next to her on the bed. "Maybelline. That pageant was totally shitty and you know it. Think about it. If you had stayed, you would've had to do the swimsuit competition. You don't seem like the kind of girl who wants to have her body judged by a bunch of strangers. You have other things going for you."

31

D. A. MacQuin

"I don't know what I'm doing."

He didn't understand why she allowed herself to be victimized over something as trivial as a beauty pageant. He didn't want to say anything, but her dad seemed like a total redneck, like those guys in high school who'd terrorize him in gym class.

"You shouldn't let your dad make you feel so bad. Do you really think he has everything figured out?"

"I suppose not. It's just shitty when your dad's disappointed in you. Everyone wants their parents to like them."

"How old are you, Maybelline?"

"Nineteen. And you?"

"Thirty. You don't think I'm too old for you, do you?"

She wiped away her tears and looked him in the eye. "I think you're perfect."

"No girl's ever said that to me before."

"I'm not like most girls."

"I can see that."

"No, I mean seriously." He waited for her to elaborate, wondering how serious her revelations could be. "I feel like I should probably tell you that I had a nervous breakdown last summer. I'd just graduated, and I thought it would be fun to look around the attic for old yearbooks with my parents in them. When I was up there, I found my mom's diary in a box. I started reading it, and she wrote all about how she seriously considered having an abortion when she was pregnant with me. She was only my age when she found out she was pregnant. She said she felt doomed to stay in Dale with my dad, whom she didn't even like very much. She called him a moron in many of the entries. She was angry as hell that she couldn't follow through with her plan of moving out to L.A. with her best friend, Olivia. When I read this, I felt like my life had no meaning, like I wasn't meant to be here. I wouldn't leave my bedroom for days. But it was worse than just depression. It was like something clicked in my brain and I could swear that I was hearing my father's voice in my head. It was kinda like in *VALIS* when Horselover Fat feels like he's perceiving two realities at once. I thought of that book a lot during this time, which is why I was so shocked when I saw your quilt. *VALIS* was such an important book to me, and it was amazing to see your quilt."

"What sort of stuff did you hear in your head?"

32

"My dad's thoughts. At random moments I heard him say that he'd wish I'd never been born, that his life would've been easier without me, and how I was a miserable little troll next to my mother. She was very beautiful, you know. For the first time in my life, I blew up at him and told him that he made everyone's life miserable and that he's a moron. I told him that they should've aborted me or put me up for adoption because my life is shit. Next thing I know, I'm being forced by orderlies to the Southern Shawnee Center. Do you know what that place is?"

He nodded. "Yes, I've heard of it."

The Southern Shawnee Center was notorious when a news story revealed the year before that they still practice shock therapy. On occasion while growing up, there would be alerts on the news whenever a patient would escape. It didn't happen often, but whenever it did, imaginations would ignite about mad men in straightjackets showing up in your back yard, staring in through your windows during dinner.

"My dad told them I threatened to kill myself, but I didn't exactly say that. He was full of shit."

"I'm sorry he did that." He felt himself begin to hate Frank.

"It wasn't a big deal, really. I just had to go to a bunch of meetings. I wasn't there very long, and as soon as I got back I went back to normal. I think I just had a weird nervous breakdown that made my brain work differently. At least that's my theory. You're the only person I've ever told about the voices in my head."

There were many times when he questioned his own sanity, especially when it came to feeling optimistic about fitting into society. It didn't seem normal to have nothing to look forward to. And he'd had his fair share of depressive episodes, especially after the deaths of his mother and grandmother. But he'd never heard voices in his head or anything close to that. He couldn't deny that her description of hearing voices, albeit temporarily, was disturbing. He'd read in the DSM IV that that could be a sign of schizophrenia. Or maybe it was a type of echolalia, he thought.

Was he lying to himself? Is it a liability to love someone who's mentally ill? He thought of all the dates he'd been on with women over the years who easily dismissed him. It made him feel damaged, as if he didn't fit into the human race. It was the worst feeling in the world— unrequited affection for reasons beyond his control. He was tired of it.

33

Seeing her so tiny and hurt, clutching a teddy bear, he now realized that he would not dismiss her. He would not throw away the possibility of love with an imperfect, but honest being—a woman brave enough to reveal her vulnerability. He felt no inclination to hide that he was seeing a psychiatrist, which felt refreshing for a change. He now viewed her with admiration because most people try to hide anything remotely unattractive about themselves. Her iconoclastic nature seemed to match his own.

"What do you want to do with your life?" he asked. "I mean, what are your life goals and dreams?"

"I don't know. In the immediate future I should probably go to college, but I can't afford it and I don't know what I'd major in. All I know is that I gotta get out of here." She gestured towards the living room where her dad bellowed loudly at some TV show. "He's driving me nuts."

"You could move in with me."

She sat upright with wide eyes. "Move in with you?" She looked optimistic yet skeptical. "I don't know…" As her voice trailed off, he detected ambivalence in her eyes and it excited him. "It is a little odd that we don't know each other. At all."

The importance of the moment had reached fruition. He thought of the scene in *Dune* when Paul Atreides addresses the Fremen desert people as their leader, laying out the plan for their uprising and survival.

He took a deep breath and continued, "I live alone in an old Victorian house in the center of Linwood. My father died when I was three, and I was raised by my ma and grandma. My ma died when I was in high school, and my granma just died last year. I inherited the house, and a good load of money. I guess I don't know exactly what I'm doing with my life either, but meanwhile I spend my time quilting and reading. I've always been a big reader. In high school I was captain of the debate team. Sometimes I take college classes in Art or English Literature. I'm in therapy. Twice a month I talk to a doctor, mainly just to talk to someone. So how about you?"

"I was born and raised in Dale. My parents split up when I was thirteen, and my mom left us for California to break into movies. She used to call every now and then, but then she just quit. Dad gets drunk and talks about how much of a whore she was, and sometimes he looks at me with this disgusted expression, like he's really looking at her. I've never been popular and I only had one boyfriend—that one over there in the prom picture. He broke my heart. Left me for a cheerleader."

"There's nothing worse than unrequited love." He took her hands. "Come with me, Maybelline. It'll be like you're moving in with your boyfriend. There's nothing wrong with that." At this exact moment, he was reminded of Amy, his old friend from high school. When they first started hanging out, she was shy and intellectually insecure; he had the feeling that he was the first person who was interested in her opinions. He discovered that she was smart, and told her as much. So she started studying more, and eventually garnered the courage to move to New York by herself to study design. He often wondered what would've happened to Amy if they hadn't become friends, because she seemed unable to look beyond the confines of dating and caring what others thought of her. Now he was presented with a similar opportunity of being able to jar open doors of perception for Maybelline—to see beyond the efforts of a beauty pageant or living in Dale with an emotionally abusive father. He didn't have everything figured out, but at least he felt free. If he could share his freedom with someone else, then he knew he was doing something right. Any considerations about her mental health were irrelevant in relation to this.

Most people would scoff at the idea of starting a relationship with a stranger, but when they looked into each other's eyes, they felt an ineffable bond that came from feeling like strangers among everyone else.

"Henry?"

"Yes?"

"Let's get outta here. I want you to walk out the front door and wait for me in your car. I'll be out in ten minutes with my things."

"What about your dad?"

"I can handle him."

"What are you going to say to him?"

"The truth. I don't want to live with him anymore. I'm a legal adult so I can do what I want."

"Will he be mad?"

"He's always been mad at me and he always will be."

"Well...if you're sure, then let's do this."

He leaned over and kissed her softly and slowly, feeling his heart swell with a feeling he hadn't felt in years. His therapist told him that people create their own destiny. He now believed this was true. Here he was, changing the course of his life while sitting on top of a quilt that he pieced together with his own hands.

Revelations

"Jesus Christ, I wish they'd leave already," Martha Valente said as she stood before her full-length mirror. She wore a white, one-piece swimsuit and combed her silky black hair that graced her thin waist. She was by far the best-looking girl in school, despite her frumpy name. People often remarked that she was way too hot to have such an old lady's name.

Her best friend, Samantha Bright, sat on the bed cleaning large, hairy buds of pot by removing the stems and seeds—a recently acquired skill from Martha.

Both girls were anxious for Martha's parents to leave for a medical conference in L.A. Dr. Valente was a neurosurgeon, and it was common knowledge that he and his wife often flew to different cities—sometimes out of the country—for conferences, leaving Martha alone at home. It seemed like a crazy thing to do, not that anyone complained. Martha Valente was a party girl. Lots of people at school vied for her friendship so they might get invited to her parties.

"Will you put some water in this, Sam?" Martha handed her a small bong made of dark purple plastic.

"Sure," said Samantha, stepping into the bathroom.

Having learned the basics of pot smoking, Samantha filled the bong with cold water. Martha taught her that it cools the temperature of the smoke, making it less harsh on your throat when you inhale.

There was tapping at the door. "We're leaving now," her mother said from the other side.

Martha opened the door to give her a quick hug. "Bye, Mom. Have a nice trip."

"Have a good trip," said Samantha, stepping out of the bathroom, leaving the bong behind, of course.

"Be careful girls," said Mrs. Valente in the proper parental tone. "And don't forget— our hotel number's on the refrigerator door if you need anything."

"Don't worry, we'll be fine," said Martha.

Samantha found it odd that Mrs. Valente initially said goodbye through the door, as if she didn't care if she saw her daughter before leaving. And why didn't her father bother to say goodbye? There was something unsettling about Martha's parents. They were successful and worldly, yet they left their beautiful, seventeen-year-old daughter alone in their expensive house for days at a time. Martha previously brushed off Samantha's questions by saying, "I make the High Honor Roll every quarter, which proves to them that I'm responsible." It never ceased to amaze Samantha the way rich parents let their kids run wild as long as nothing serious presented itself. It seemed obvious that Martha was the type of kid who could engage in illicit activities (such as the ones they had planned for that evening) and not get caught.

"You're not gonna believe the new swimsuit I just bought," said Martha. "I've been dying to put this on." She disappeared into her bathroom.

"Cool. I'm gonna go downstairs and put on some music. See 'ya down there."

Samantha played King Crimson—a band Martha recently got her into, and sauntered around the living room, admiring the beautiful objects the Valentes acquired during their extensive travels. She recently moved with her mother, Maybelline, to Westchester because they wanted a fresh start away from Manhattan. They left after her father, the artist Henry Bright, died in a car accident. He was taking a cab home from his retrospective at the Folk Art Museum in Manhattan when a drunk driver slammed into the side of the cab where he was sitting. Both drivers died as well. Some said it was ironic that he died on the night that his life's work was honored.

So far things worked out well for Samantha. It was the first quarter of her Junior year, and already she had befriended the most popular girl in school. On top of this, her new boyfriend, Paul, was the best buddy of Martha's boyfriend. The guys planned to come over later and no doubt spend the night. Eli, Martha's boyfriend, was bringing over ecstasy.

Samantha wasn't crazy about Paul, but she appreciated the social cache of going on double dates with Martha. She recently lost her virginity to Paul, more as a perfunctory task than an act of affection. It seemed like something to get out of the way as she basked in the sexual power she held over him. His desperate infatuation with her was more intoxicating than her feelings towards him.

At her old prep school on the Upper East Side, Samantha was familiar with the fast crowd—the pretty girls who had fake I.D.s and went out to clubs on weekends. Half the time they didn't get carded because the clubs like having hot girls around. Samantha never hung out with the partiers and druggies, in part because she was only a freshman at the time. Plus, her parents were strict. She felt distinctly different from her friends in this regard; she was the only one whose parents were small town people from the Midwest, and had middle class values because they were newly rich.

Back in the late nineties, Samantha's father, Henry Bright, made a name for himself in the art world by creating off beat, elaborate quilts—some that were massively large. His quilting technique was hailed as unique, and he combined elements of sequential narrative, and multi-textured fabrics. After his first big Manhattan opening, the *Times* called his work "oddly post-modern" due to his reverence of ancient iconic imagery that's aesthetically analogous to pixel art in a folk art medium. Henry Bright created buzz as an artist who bridged high and low art.

After the accident, Maybelline spent more time with friends from the art world that lived in Westchester. Samantha was glad to leave because she was concerned that her mother was becoming unhinged in the city. She began making more of her signature specious statements, which she and her dad were subjected to on various occasions. Maybelline was famous for stating things in a non sequitur-like fashion, as if she were privy to the Fates.

"Well, what do you think?" said Martha as she descended the staircase with a huge grin. She wore a light pink string bikini that barely supported her ample breasts.

"You look totally hot."

"Wait—this is the best part!"

She turned around to reveal a g-string bikini, her round, taut buttocks proudly on display. Both girls squealed with laughter.

"Oh my god! Martha—you little slut!"

Turning her head back over her shoulder she replied, "There's no way in hell I'd let my parents see me in this! Eli's gonna freak out."

Clad in their bikinis, Martha and Samantha relaxed in the pool on rafts, carefully passing the bong back and forth. The Valente's pool was kidney shaped, and surrounded by groomed plants and flowers.

"I can't wait for the guys to get here," Martha said. "Eli always gets good shit. He knows this girl at NYU who deals right out of her dorm room."

"That's pretty stupid."

"I know. You'd think she'd at least meet people at a coffee shop or something." Martha yawned and stretched with a satisfied smirk on her face. She added in a dreamy voice, "Eli is so hot."

"Yeah, he's a great looking guy."

"But I don't know what he'll do after high school. Seems like he can only do three things: get drugs, fuck, and make cheeseburgers."

Samantha giggled. "Everyone loves a good cheeseburger."

"So are you gonna dose with us tonight or what?"

"I don't know… probably."

Samantha was secretly elated about her adventures with Martha. She never did drugs when she lived in the city, but if Martha Valente could party, then it couldn't be truly wrong due to her obvious intelligence. At school, Samantha noticed that the teachers treated Martha with respect. It was typical for rich kids to get better treatment, but there was something special about Martha. Samantha had never met anyone so gorgeous, well spoken, and well read.

She also noticed that Martha was nonchalant about intimidating a lot of people. One day when they were getting high in Martha's SUV on their lunch hour, Martha made her laugh so hard that soda almost came out her nose. They were talking about all the jealous rumors that float around about her. She said, "Only the best people are ridiculed. Look what happened to Jesus." She always said things like this with a straight face; she said it was gauche to laugh at your own jokes.

It was ironic that since Samantha started smoking pot, drinking, and having sex, her grades had never been higher. This is what made her realize how important competition was for achievement; she had to keep up with Martha. But the dark side to feeling great about popularity and good grades was feeling deep remorse. How could she be happy when her dad hadn't been gone a year yet?

"I'm really glad you moved here."

"So am I."

"The last time I had a close female friend was in the fifth grade."

"Really, why?

Martha shrugged. "I had a best friend but she moved away."

"That's too bad."

"I have some friends, but I feel like they're always comparing themselves to me and trying to tear me down."

"Yeah, I noticed that. They're just jealous. My dad taught me that it's insecure people who put others down."

"Sounds like he was pretty cool."

"He was."

"Well, I'm just glad you're not like that. Of course it helps that you're totally hot."

"You're totally hot."

"No, you're totally hot."

"Did you hear the doorbell?" asked Samantha.

Martha glanced at her waterproof watch. "It's too early for the boys. I wonder who it is."

They got out of the pool, wrapped themselves with towels, and went inside. Martha made sure to place the bong behind a plant.

"Oh shit," said Martha, giggling like crazy after looking through the front window. "It's a couple of those Jehovah Witness boys." The familiar look of mischief crept across her lovely face. "Should we let 'em in?" she asked softly.

They could barely contain their laughter. "Why not?" said Samantha. "It might be funny."

Martha whipped both of their towels off and opened the door. Samantha felt embarrassed for a moment, but if Martha could stand there in a g-string, then she could wear her bikini without covering up.

"Hello," said Martha.

"Good afternoon! We're with the Jehovah's Witnesses. My name is Theodore, and this is Luke. We'd like to discuss some Bible literature with you. May we come in and speak with you for a moment?"

"Sure!" she said cheerfully, stepping aside. "Come in."

The boys entered the house, straining to appear oblivious to the fact that the girls wore bikinis. Theodore looked agitated as he scratched his scraggly attempt at a beard while Luke was wide-eyed and jittery, like a child being sent to the principal's office.

"Would you mind coming out to the pool?" asked Martha.

"That would be fine," said Theodore.

As Martha led the group through the house, Samantha quickly glanced back to see the look on the boys' faces. She sensed the powerful effect they had on the boys. Paul and Eli are gonna crack up at this, she thought.

Luke was one of Martha's many admirers; she was often the focus of his masturbatory fantasies—in some she was dressed like Valeria from *Conan the Barbarian*. He had no idea she lived in this house. Even though he'd had classes with her since junior high, he suspected that she didn't recognize him at all. He felt paranoid, as if she knew his dirty secret. His heart raced, and he couldn't believe what he was now seeing—her nearly naked body in all its glory, just as he imagined. Such big breasts, and that bottom—what heavenly curves, he thought. And Samantha's really pretty too. She was the talk of the school—the pretty new blond girl who was Martha's new best friend. *Jesus, please help me to be strong.*

"Have a seat," said Martha, gesturing towards patio furniture situated under a large umbrella. She then dove into the pool and reclined on her raft, with Samantha following suit.

"Thank you for letting us in," said Luke.

"No problem. By the way, I'm Martha, and this is Samantha."

"Nice to meet both of you," said Luke. He caught himself staring, so he looked away, glancing instead at his surroundings— potted plants, a plastic bucket filled with pool supplies, a barbeque grill. He wished his family had a pool—the water looked fantastic in the heat.

Theodore also tried to not stare too much at the girls. Their skimpy swimsuits irritated him, as did his itchy face. Sparse, dark stubble peppered his cheeks and chin as he attempted to grow a beard. His girlfriend, Elizabeth, told him she was attracted to men who resembled Jesus.

He opened his bag and pulled out some pamphlets, dropping a few on the ground. After replacing them in his bag, he held one up that had the words "Behold the Good News!" on the front. In an awkward and falsely enthusiastic voice he said, "We're here to talk about the good news about faith in Jesus. Do you know what we mean by 'good news'?"

"No," Martha flatly replied, while Samantha shook her head.

In his bland voice, Theodore continued, "The good news is that by having faith in Jesus Christ as your Lord and Savior, you will have everlasting life."

There was a moment of silence as Martha regarded him blankly. She wore big Jackie O. sunglasses that hid her true expression, but her mouth formed a slight smirk. Samantha felt uneasy, sensing the tension almost like a physical presence. Then she wanted to giggle suddenly when she imagined herself and Martha as sirens in the water, luring wayward men to crash.

Breaking the awkward silence, Luke asked, "Were you ladies raised Christian?" The girls nodded.

Theodore intoned, "Then I'm sure you're familiar with this message. But our mission to remind people to have faith in Jesus is because we believe we're living in a crucial time period. Our faith emphasizes that we're now living in end times. We have some literature here that explains this." He held up another pamphlet that said, "The End Time is Among Us."

"Why do you believe we're living in end times?" asked Martha.

"We believe the signs are clear," Theodore replied with authority, "due to the prevalence of violence in the world—the increase of rape, kidnapping, murder, and other brutal crimes. According to Matthew, Chapter Twenty-four, verse twelve, 'And because lawlessness will abound, the love of many will grow cold. But he who endures to the end shall be saved.'"

"I'm sorry," said Martha, "but I don't see how taking a quote from the Bible proves that we're living in end times. Sure, there's a lot of violence in the world, but when hasn't there been? How can you quantitatively measure violence in the world throughout the history of mankind?"

Theodore looked flustered, which didn't surprise Luke. Every once in a while, they were let inside so somebody could argue with them, sometimes for entertainment. This didn't bother Luke nearly as much as Theodore. Luke felt that some people believe what they want to believe and there's not much they could do about it. One time, an old man listened patiently to Theodore's sermon, then all of a sudden blew up at them and started raving about how they were foolish and uninformed for not realizing that aliens once lived on Earth who facilitated evolution and agriculture—two things they weren't discussing.

Theodore wiped sweat off his brow with a handkerchief and continued, "Our point is that through faith, Jehovah grants everlasting life. And those that are wicked and non-believing will be condemned."

Luke sensed that this was a disaster. Samantha looked bored, while Martha was on the attack. I have to admit, thought Luke, Martha makes a good point about "End Times." He realized that he and Theodore disagreed about certain core beliefs of their faith. Theodore took the Bible literally, while he preferred to preach on the goodness of the gospel and how it affects daily lives.

"What do you mean by 'wicked'?" asked Martha in an irritated tone.

Theodore took a deep breath and continued, "The wicked are those that don't follow Jehovah's word, which is why our message is important. We believe that the Bible teaches us to impart good judgment and soundness of mind to make wise decisions. For example, by not associating with certain people, we're less likely to be in the wrong place at the wrong time." He looked at Martha when he said this.

The emphasis on the phrase "certain people" rubbed Martha the wrong way. Even Luke thought he sounded off-putting. After all, there were rumors around school that Martha was fast and liked to do drugs. Theodore was wary of wealthy people.

Martha flipped over onto her stomach, revealing her glorious, round buttocks. The seams of the raft had created slight, vertical lines in her flesh. Her face was defiant as she dared them to be tempted. This was when Luke felt that familiar throb in his shorts. Oh no...not now, he thought.

Martha said to Theodore, "I believe that wickedness is a subjective term. I thought Jesus was the only judge."

This caught Luke's attention. She really is smart, he thought, not that he was surprised. He knew how fast she could turn in an Algebra exam and get an "A." At this point, his excitement was uncontrollable. He had no choice but to sit with his legs together and lean forward a bit.

"What I mean by 'wicked' or 'bad'," said Theodore, "is when people aren't aware of Christian ethics."

"Wait a second," said Martha. "You think Christianity is the only form of ethics? Does this mean that people from other countries where Christianity isn't prevalent are all sinners? What about Buddhism, which is largely consistent with Christ's teachings? Are

Buddhists wrong even though their ethics are practically the same as Christians?"

Luke politely interjected, "We don't want to judge other religions. We just think the wisdom and truth of Christian faith becomes apparent through practice." He heard himself speak, but didn't recognize his rote, robotic tone.

Samantha noticed Martha seething under her sunglasses. Martha mentioned having beef with some Christian girls at school who gossiped and snickered about her behind her back.

"You know what?" said Martha to Theodore, sensing that he was the more hard core Christian of the two, "I've read the Bible and I know what it says. But don't you get that you're just structuring your faith in an ideology? I think Christianity is great—I'm totally down with J.C., which I believe is a personal matter. I think it's annoying when certain Christians have to advertise how good they are. For instance, look at that Elizabeth Charles girl at school. That frumpy girl who dresses like she's down with J.C. Penney's—"

"Wait a second," said Theodore. "Elizabeth is my girlfriend and I won't have you talking—"

"Here me out!" said Martha. "She calls herself a Christian, but she's judgmental and racist. Are you aware that your girlfriend makes racist comments about me being Cuban? I can hear her when I walk down the hall."

Theodore didn't know how to respond. Luke remained silent as well. He knew Martha was telling the truth.

"I'm sorry, but mere faith in Jesus doesn't cut it with me," Martha continued. "Besides, how do you explain all the horrible and random things that happen to people every day? Look at what happened to Samantha's dad last year—he was on his way home from a museum and was killed by a drunk driver. He was a Christian. Where was Jesus when that happened?"

Samantha was surprised that she'd bring up her dad. But she didn't say anything. She was high and the heat was getting to her brain.

In a calm voice, Luke asked Samantha, "Were you angry with Jesus when this happened?"

"I don't know... I was mad at everything when it happened. Why?"

Theodore said to her, "The Bible teaches that Jehovah will

provide divine protection for those that have faith by either removing a harmful situation, or giving us the strength to endure it."

"Well, that sounds pretty convenient," said Samantha. "So in other words, regardless if you have faith or not, it doesn't change anything."

"That's not exactly what I'm saying. You see—"

"You Bible thumpers make me sick! You think you have everything figured out. It's all bullshit. The world is chaos! People like you walk around preaching faith so you can feel better about yourselves."

Samantha surprised herself. She was lashing out at every inappropriate gesture of condolence ever uttered to her. All the talk of Heaven, faith, and Jesus was nothing more than an opiate to her, just like Marx said in that book Martha let her borrow.

"I think we better leave," said Theodore as he gathered up his things. "We don't have time for these Jezebels."

"Theodore! That's not right. Apologize," said Luke.

"I'll apologize when she apologizes for insulting Elizabeth."

Martha smiled large and said, "Fuck you, Bible thumper."

Theodore shook his head. "Let's get out of here."

Luke noticed Samantha looking right at him. It made him feel shame; a beautiful girl like her could only view him as a religious freak. He saw Martha staring at Theodore and holding in laughter. This made him think about Elizabeth, whom he's heard make disparaging comments about Martha, other minorities, and Catholics too. Elizabeth considered herself the paragon of chastity, but he knew for a fact that she gave Theodore hand jobs on a regular basis.

"You can stay, Luke," said Samantha. She thought it was charming the way he attempted to hide his erection earlier. It was then that she realized he was cute. His friend, however, was an obnoxious asshole and she wanted to punish him. She'd learned from Martha that it drives people nuts when you ignore them.

"You can totally stay," said Martha. "Jump in—the water feels great."

Luke could no longer convince himself that Theodore was still his best friend. His judgmental attitude was getting lame, and his girlfriend was a bitch. He'd always love Jesus, but he'd grown out of Theodore's world of proselytizing. He was tired of worrying about people making fun of them when they made their rounds, and feeling doubtful about the mandate of chastity before marriage.

"I'm staying," he said.

"Fine. Do what you want. Just try not to catch anything."

The girls laughed at him as Luke peeled off his clothes to his boxer shorts and dove in. It felt like he was being baptized for a second time. "Sorry about him," he said, after Theodore was gone.

"What's his problem?" Martha asked.

Luke shrugged. "He needs to lose his virginity bad."

"What about you? What do you need?" Martha swam towards him while Samantha followed her lead. They cornered him in the shallow end.

He laughed nervously. He couldn't believe he was hanging out with Martha Valente and Samantha, the hot new blond girl at school everyone was talking about. "Umm...I don't know." He sensed the importance of the moment, but was too tongue-tied to play along.

"You're cute," said Samantha.

"Totally." Martha ran her hands through his hair. "Feel how soft his hair is."

Samantha stroked his head and looked at Martha's mischievous face, indicating that they were thinking the same thing. "Hey, I've got an idea," said Samantha. "Let's play a game. Close your eyes, and try to guess which one of us is kissing you."

"Um... okay."

He shut his eyes and Samantha kissed him long and slow. When she finished, she pointed to his crotch and silently laughed. He was almost poking out of his boxer shorts. "Okay, who was that?"

"I don't know... was it Martha?"

"Wrong!" They yelled.

"Oops," he said. They thought his flushed cheeks and nervousness was adorable.

"Let's do it again," said Martha.

He shut his eyes, and this time Martha kissed him slowly with lots of tongue. She reached down and pulled him out of his boxers. "Oh! Um, hehehe..."

"Keep your eyes closed," Martha whispered.

When he couldn't stand it any longer, he opened his eyes and stuffed himself back into his boxers. "I really don't know who that was." His voice cracked and his cheeks burned even redder. The girls looked at each other and smiled. The decision was made.

It was cool and gusty out when Samantha returned home the next day. She went straight to her room and lay down in bed, still exhausted from being up late partying. Paul told her that if she smoked some pot later, some of the effects of ecstasy would re-enter her system, triggering a nice rush.

She wasn't sure if her mom was home; she was still getting used to the little creaks the house naturally made when no one was around. She turned on her side and watched the wind blow leaves against her window, making her nostalgic for fall. Martha's pool would be closed in a few days and soon the weather would demand a shopping trip for new clothes. She heard it was much colder there than in the city.

It was a blast partying with Martha, Eli, and Paul. But the little fling with Luke in the afternoon might have been a bit much. It was the first time she'd fooled around with two guys in one day. She didn't go all the way with Luke, but she suspected he felt a little less like a virgin after spending some time alone with him in the guest bedroom. It thrilled her to see the ecstatic look on his face as he indulged in physical pleasure for what seemed like the first time. She imagined layers of religious brainwashing being stripped away in his mind. It made her feel proud.

The garage door opened and shut, filling her with a rush of paranoia. She was no longer convinced that her mom wasn't aware of her new lifestyle habits. Maybelline hadn't said anything, but now the silence between them was disturbing. Her new freedom to stay out late and spend nights at Martha's house whenever she wanted was never debated. She assumed her mom would snap out of her indifference eventually, but now she wondered.

There was a light rapping at the door. Maybelline entered with a solemn expression that put Samantha at ease.

"Did you have a good time at Martha's?"

"Yeah, sure."

"Listen, I want to chat a little about something."

"Sure, have a seat."

Maybelline sat on the edge of the bed, looked out the window with a distant expression and said, "I just want to say… change for the better will happen when you learn to forgive." She took a deep breath, gave Samantha a little half smile, then made her way towards the door.

"Wait. That's it?"

Maybelline's brows were raised quizzically. "Yes, that's all I had to say, Sweetie."

Samantha's irritation rose quickly as it did with the Jehovah's Witness boy. For as long as she could remember, she and her dad had to listen to her otherworldly comments, which smacked of rural quirkiness from back home in Southern Illinois. They'd laugh a little and make some comment about how eccentric she was. Right now it didn't feel quirky or eccentric. It was annoying. Maybelline drifted from day to day in a haze since they left the city, and now this all of a sudden.

"What does that mean? How do you expect me to respond to that?"

"I'm sorry, I didn't mean to upset you. I don't know what you want me to say."

"I want you to say something!"

Maybelline sighed. "Let's talk about this later."

"Fine, whatever."

After the door was shut, she lay back down and stared at the glass flowered light fixture on the ceiling. She was always skeptical of her mom's supposed "psychic ability." But her dad was a believer. She remembered something he told her to calm her nervousness on her first day of school in New York. He said, "Remember to look backwards and forward at the same time... and remember who you are. I know it sounds hokey, but this is what your mom told me when I was preparing for my first gallery show in Chicago. She knew that by not forgetting my roots I would succeed. It was the biggest inspiration in my life. She knew my quilts were going to lead to New York, and look where we are now—just two blocks from Central Park!"

Samantha pondered this and admitted that sometimes her mom did just know things. This made her remember the night of her dad's death—something she hadn't thought of in a while, as if the part of her mind that controls sanity prevented it. That night Maybelline cried and pleaded with her dad to leave his show at the American Folk Art Museum early, creating a mild scene. Even Samantha thought her mom was being weird and paranoid. It chilled her to remember being slightly pissed at her mom for being embarrassing on such an important night. And now, her mom was probably devastated knowing that she could have saved his life that night. The fact that this was the first time the thought occurred to Samantha made her roll over on her side and cry hard into her hands. She felt like a terrible, selfish person.

She wiped her tears and let her mind settle on the debauchery from yesterday. It was Martha's idea to fool around with Luke; she said it would be good practice. She now asked herself, when did I become someone who uses others for practice? Then she wondered how discreet Paul and Eli would be about them all doing drugs and having sex in front of each other. It wasn't technically "group sex," but it was intimate and intense enough to make her feel like they weren't typical high school juniors. Last night she didn't care about anything but how the surreal quality of it all made her special in some way, on Martha's level.

Thinking of all this made her feel stuck in a mental rut. She dreaded going to school on Monday to face her friends, as well as Luke. What if rumors floated around school about how slutty she was? Why did this not occur to her last night? This was the last thought she had before drifting into a deep, troubled sleep—one that compensated for the lost hours of rest that drinking and ecstasy took from her. Her dreams were lucid, with vivid scenes of anger directed mainly at herself. Martha was a villain and a saint, and her mom was a powerful figure demanding respect while projecting vulnerability. She felt her mother's pain in the dream; she found herself seeing things from her point of view, but as an elderly woman at the end of her life, sitting alone at home. In her mother's voice she thought: I've missed Henry every second of every day since he left, and when I die, his presence will be with me till my very last breath.

When she awoke, she pondered the intensity of her parent's love for each other, and realized that the drastic change in her behavior that Martha catalyzed was pure distraction. She was distracting herself from grasping the reality of her mom's situation, from being angry at her for being distant, and mostly she distracted herself from being angry at the chaotic universe.

She needed to forgive her mom for coping with the loss of her life partner the best way she knew how, and forgive herself for coping the best she could. It was a plan that was easy to conceive because clearly her mom had forgiven her for her transgressions.

Maybelline was correct: when Samantha looked into the past and the future, she realized that with forgiveness, things would get better.

Across The Ocean

It was impossible to not think of *Fantasy Island* when our little plane swooped down over the blue-green water to land on the tiny island of Piliguet. It was my first time visiting a tropical region, unlike my co-worker, Oliver, who was peacefully slumped down next to me. He had the amazing ability to shut off his consciousness when he wasn't preoccupied with talking about himself.

This was Oliver's second trip to Piliguet. He was used to long plane rides—his office displayed photos of him and his sexy blond girlfriend skiing in British Columbia, basking on a Caribbean beach, sitting in a café in Prague. It impressed me that he was only twenty-nine and already a senior stock analyst. When he started at McClary Capital fresh out of grad school, the company was a small startup. Oliver said on the plane that he and some of the other analysts had no idea that the company would grow from a two million to a two billion dollar hedge fund in just five years. He said this with a sly smile, as if they'd joined the best fraternity for getting laid. These were the guys who were always picked first to be on a team in gym class, and the ones who cracked up when they could make you fall by wacking your running legs as hard as they could during dodge ball.

When we stepped off the plane, the 109-degree heat bombarded my lungs, almost making me gasp. We made our way to the baggage claim, where we spotted a small man who held up our names. He led us to his gray limousine and drove us to the Piliguet Resort. I rolled down the window to get air on my face as we drove down the coastal road. The fresh sea air lessened my lingering nausea from the turbulent flight.

Oliver looked relaxed and cool as ever. He was one of those annoyingly handsome guys with "all American good looks." Tall and athletic with green eyes and strawberry blond hair. When he was fifteen he was cast in a pimple medicine commercial; while it was being filmed on his prep school campus, the cameraman picked him out of a crowd as he was walking to lacrosse practice. Millions of hormonal American boys bought the product so they could look like

51

Oliver. He was so good looking that I wondered if he cheated on his girlfriend because it was obvious that he could if he wanted to. And frankly, he seemed like the type of guy who would. I told myself to not be envious. I guess my mind doesn't work that way anyway. I was used to being friends with the handsome guy. This is why I'm "the smart guy"—the Spock to some other guy's Kirk.

My friend Jake was the one who exposed me to the mentality of a confident male who could easily get women. "It's easy," he once told me after a disparaging night out in Cambridge. "They like it if you're aloof—almost snobby, because it makes them think you have something to be snobby about. And it makes them feel special that you're paying attention to them." We were at one of those college bars populated by Harvard and MIT kids. Where do you go? What's your major? Where are you from? These were the ubiquitous and inoffensive pickup lines. They worked if the girl was attracted to you physically, and they didn't if she preferred to scan the room for someone better. You could tell this was the case when you were talking to a girl and her eyes didn't really focus on you. Instead, they'd dart around the room as she generated a polite exit strategy.

In college I was interested in starting off with smart, nerdy looking girls. The ones with tortoise shell frame glasses and figures that maybe weren't as refined as the athletes and debutante types who wore bright trendy clothes. I thought maybe the nerd girls were more like me—the best and brightest in their class who studied hard and sacrificed to be at a great school. I was the first in the history of my high school to make it to Harvard. When Jake and I first moved there, he said I should go for some fluffy blond type, just for the hell of it. He reasoned that I might as well see what it's like, since they're usually more slutty, and it might be fun to try something I've never done before, "because that's what college is all about." It's funny how he always proclaimed to know what college was "all about." He moved across the country with me to Cambridge to get a job and start a new life— not to attend college like me. He was never interested in school. "You're at Harvard, man. That's something special," he'd say, drunkenly jabbing his index finger into my bony chest. "You deserve the best." His confidence was born in our small, insignificant town in Southern Illinois, but it was better than nothing, albeit a skewed confidence formed in relation to rural simplicity. It's not the same as being a blue blood from Connecticut like Oliver, but Jake still had something.

On the plane, Oliver talked about his family's wealth in a matter-of-fact way, not in a bragging way. He often spent his summers hanging out with his friends in the Hamptons. And he's dated a few models, which introduces an element of surreal partying. He and his friends were like a race of Titans who weren't required to follow the same rules as everyone else. Frank conversations about this stuff intrigued me because I didn't grow up around rich people. I grew up upper middle class, and that was more than what most people had. My dad was a small town lawyer with a great stockbroker up in Chicago. He always paid my tuition, which required years of saving and making sacrifices. I've been called "rich" with distain by redneck boys with uneducated parents who thought my dad made too much money. This was why my friendship with Jake was so great. He was the self-proclaimed "country boy" who liked guns, drove a gigantic truck, and went to all the keggers—the hallmarks of being a redneck. I could go anywhere with him and not be called a "nerd" or a "fag" like some of my other skinny friends on the debate team.

I met Jake when we were eight and playing with my Lego spaceship at recess. He thought it was cool and asked me if I had more because his dad wouldn't buy him any. I told him I had the Lego Castle at home that I got for Christmas. That's how it all started. After school, we went to my house. My mom brought glasses of milk and homemade chocolate chip cookies to my room while Jake and I built a castle together.

I think Oliver talked to me about his prep school in Massachusetts and his European vacations because he thought I had a similar background. People often assume this because of my education. I like to keep quiet and play along because it isn't necessary to tell people everything. This was easy to do because he did most of the talking on the plane, but didn't ask me many questions. I didn't mind because Oliver and everyone else at work had no idea that deep down I was nervous. It was like starting over at Cambridge again—back when I went from being Timmy to Tim.

I was new at the company, and still grasping all of the transactions in the legal department. The growth at McClary Capital entailed hiring more lawyers, "to keep everyone out of orange jump suits," as the boss liked to say. It was overwhelming, but much better than working at a large law firm. The hours weren't as long, and I was getting sick of working primarily with other lawyers. It seemed that so many of us had forgotten why we became attorneys in the first place as we worked like automatons reviewing documents for large corporations. One night I was in a shitty mood after being at work for fourteen hours straight for the third consecutive day. I felt loopy and started asking some of my colleagues what made them go to law school in the first place (It was normal at work to act nutty when you feel dead inside.) At least ninety percent of them said something like, "I don't know... it just seemed like a good thing to do... I thought it might lead to something." I was part of this ninety percent who felt that the work hadn't yet led to anything.

"Are you feeling better?" asked Oliver.

"Yeah, much better. Thanks."

"You know what? This makes the Bahamas look like shit. I can't wait to hit the beach."

We drove along a stretch of blue-green water and powdery light sand. There were a few small hotels that rented parasailing equipment and beach umbrellas. But none of these places would be as nice as Piliguet Resort, the "most exquisite resort-hotel on the island," as their brochure stated. The owner of the resort defaulted on a large loan from us, so we were sent here to assess the condition of the property as a moneymaker, and complete all foreclosure proceedings.

Our boss, Regan McClary, was incredibly excited about the project. The projections were good, and the American dollar went a long way in Piliguet. It was a small island measuring three miles from one side to the other. So far, it looked like there was much room for development. Regan envisioned tourism on par with Key West, but more exotic. He wanted to expand into snorkeling, scuba diving tours, glass bottom boats, bicycle and moped rentals, perhaps an expansion into upscale restaurants, and a monster Madison Avenue ad campaign that would make all of this happen. Regan founded his company only five years ago, and already saw himself as king of a tropical island.

"I've never been to the Bahamas."

"You should totally go—it's a lot of fun."

I wasn't well traveled because I never had the time. Right after high school it was Harvard, Harvard Law, then Crandall & Rothman in New York... my life hadn't gotten to the level of hanging out in

Prague cafes with pretty blond girls despite being a decent looking thirty-four-year-old lawyer. As I pondered this, I felt even better that I was now at a hedge fund. Sure, there was an element of roteness in the work, and I wouldn't say I was passionate about reviewing every detail of a deal as if my life depended on it, always maintaining a compliance environment to avoid trouble with the SEC, always following the money and verifying facts via consistent emails and phone calls. It gave me headaches getting used to this type of work, but the payoff and freedom was worth it. Follow the money indeed.

The car pulled into the resort's red brick driveway where we were greeted by the owner, Mr. Toma. He was a small brown man of about fifty, dressed in a floral patterned shirt and baggy shorts. He was surprisingly obsequious for a man who was about to hand over the ownership of his resort. Perhaps he'd be happier managing rather than owning, or maybe he had made enough to retire. From the looks of the place, he must have been very well off, not that this was our concern.

The main building of the resort was a massive colonial style structure. There were huts lining the property not far from the beach, and a sprawling golf course across the street. We walked through the lobby, which had a tall bamboo garden in the center encased in glass. After getting our keys at the front desk, he escorted us outside along a stone path that led to two large round huts. "I'm sure you'll find everything very comfortable," said Mr. Toma. "Please let me know if you need anything."

"Thank you," said Oliver. "Are we still having dinner tomorrow night?"

"Yes, of course. We can have dinner in the restaurant," he replied, gesturing to a glass-encased wing of the resort behind us. "Is seven all right?"

"Certainly," said Oliver.

We thanked Mr. Toma, who left us to relax.

"This is really cool," I said. "I wasn't expecting to get my own hut. I thought we were getting regular hotel rooms."

"So did I. Looks like he gave us the deluxe treatment. In the brochure it said that they have Jacuzzis in them."

"Sweet."

"I don't know about you, but I am beat."

"Me too. I think I need a nap."

"Cool. Let's meet up later and hit the beach. And if we're up to it, maybe we can get some pretty little Asian girls to come over and give us massages." He flashed his wolf grin. "Just kidding."

"Funny." As soon as I read in the brochure that there was a massage service, I knew he'd make some creepy comment about it.

My hut was a large space that had a sunken living room, a fully stocked bar, and a patio with an outdoor Jacuzzi. Gauzy mosquito netting draped over and encircled the king-sized bed, which reminded me of the bed in *Clash of the Titans* where the golden blond princess slept. That movie was on cable when I was a kid, and I used to get turned on thinking about her asleep in that bed of hers, covered with the white netting. It's funny how pre-adolescent masturbatory material can be triggered in your brain.

I opened the sliding glass door, leaving the screen closed. I splashed water on my face, stripped down to my boxers, and collapsed in bed. The soft mattress felt like heaven beneath my stiff muscles. The gentle waves of the ocean coaxed me to sleep; it was a pleasant contrast to Oliver's conversation. He's not a bad guy. But you could tell he always knew he was right, like when he talked about which stocks were going to rise or fall, or who was fucking the receptionist at work. He's also self-centered. But in a way this was endearing because I envied his satisfaction with himself, with no burden of oppressive doubt. Is lacking self-awareness the key to happiness, like when you're a kid and you don't know any better?

I've lost countless hours of sleep playing what I call the "What if" game in my tired mind. What if Jake hadn't clouded my time and judgment in college? What if we had tried harder to quit partying so much? What if I was slightly less smart and hadn't gotten into Harvard Law?

It was dusk when I awoke from my nap, remembering a dream about Jake. He was driving me home in his truck after winning a debate tournament, as he often did. In the dream, it was summertime, and I could feel the cool night air on my face and smell honey suckle in the air through the open windows. We were listening to The Pixies and passing a joint back and forth. I often have dreams where we're getting high, which makes me feel empty when I awaken. My subconscious has the tendency to equate happiness with getting high—a past happiness that can never be recovered. As an adult, you can never return to the pure moments of discovery—the memories untainted by stress or judgment. There will never be another time when you can listen to Pink Floyd, Jane's Addiction, Jimi Hendrix, Devo, The Doors, The Talking Heads, and David Bowie for the first time, while smoking pot and driving around in the country with your best friend in high school. More than anything, these dreams made me sad because I knew that in the deepest part of my mind, when I'm feeling unsettled in the world or depressed, my mind returns to him.

I put on swim trunks and a t-shirt, grabbed a towel, and walked over to Oliver's hut. He'd fastened a sign on his door that said, "At the beach." When I saw him at a distance I waved. He was walking out of the water carrying a boogie board. "The water feels great!" he called out to me. When I looked at the sky back-dropped behind the ocean, the first word that came to mind was "majestic." The clouds were gigantic and puffy against a pink, red, and orange sky. I had never seen a more dramatic sunset. It looked fake.

I jogged towards the water with a grin on my face. I threw my towel and t-shirt on the sand and dove right in, letting the warm water engulf me. I hadn't swum in the ocean since visiting Miami for a business trip four years ago. It wasn't nearly as nice as this. Here, you could walk out through clear and shallow water for several feet, and the sand felt powdery fine. I couldn't believe it was part of my job to be here.

After we exhausted ourselves swimming, we lay on our towels and looked up at the darkening sky. I felt so at peace with the world that I entertained notions of leaving the rat race and moving to some tropical paradise for good.

Oliver propped himself on his elbow and asked me, "So honestly, how do you like it at McClary so far?"

"I like it. I'm still getting the hang of things, but so far everyone seems pretty cool and easy-going. That was one thing all the attorneys emphasized when I interviewed. They all said they were happier and less stressed than they were working in-house."

"Is it?"

"Definitely. The hours aren't as long."

"They interviewed a lot of people before choosing you."

"Really?"

"Yeah, it took a long time to find someone. There were two

57

others before you who were called back for second interviews, but they didn't make the cut."

"That's interesting. I wonder why."

"I'm not sure. All I know is that when Patricia walked one woman out to the elevator after her interview, she took her fucking shoes off."

"Why did she do that?"

"I'm not sure. Patricia said she was like, 'Girl, my feet are killing me in these interview shoes. You know how it is, Girl.'"

"That's hilarious."

"It's idiotic."

"Well, I'm glad they picked me. I had to restrain myself from removing my shirt."

"Ha! That's funny. Patricia told me that all the attorneys unanimously liked you."

"That's cool." It was the first time Oliver bothered to talk about me.

"I have a confession."

"Oh yeah?" I wondered what other gossip about me he was about to divulge.

"Regan asked me to do some Internet research on you before hiring you."

"Before you say anything, let me just say that I was hungry, and the modeling agency gave me fifty dollars for the photo shoot."

"Dude, you're hilarious. No, I was gonna say that I came across a short story you published on E-manuelle.com."

"Oh…"

"I assumed it was you because the site said you were a writer for the *Harvard Crimson*, which was on your resume. So that was you, right?"

"Yes, it was."

E-manuelle.com was a popular dating website that I explored on a lark during my freshman year. I used to think that only desperate people did online dating. I pictured unattractive and overweight people sitting alone at their computers on Friday nights, knowing they couldn't meet people otherwise. I desperately wanted to differentiate myself from them, even though I had a hard time meeting girls.

This all changed when I went to a party where I had a long

conversation about free will with the teaching assistant from my Moral Reasoning class. He introduced me to his cute girlfriend, another graduate student in philosophy. When I asked them how they met, they told me without hesitation that they met on E-manuelle. This suggested that maybe I was out of touch, and perhaps it wasn't shameful to do online dating. They were both good-looking and bright, albeit a bit nerdy like me, without tons of dating experience.

When I went to the site, I discovered that it was more than just crass personal ads where people made themselves seem taller and more cool than they actually were. It also featured photography, film and book reviews, essays, and erotic short stories. I was surprised to see writing by some well-known authors that I admired. This is what convinced me to submit a story. (My freshman writing class got me thinking that I might write books or screenplays one day.) I thought it would be cool to get one of my stories published by the same website where "real" writers sent their work. This goal immediately took precedence over dating. I worked like crazy on a story about a man who doesn't realize he's been set up by his girlfriend to be seduced by a call girl because she wants to catch him cheating, and therefore have an excuse to break up with him. The free will conversation made me think of this: if the girlfriend functions as divine providence, this renders the boyfriend less deserving of moral blame.

I was nineteen when E-manuelle published my story, "The Wonder Wheel." When they contacted me with the news, I considered using a pen name due to the explicit sexual content. I wondered if the overt eroticism would embarrass me later on. I talked it over with Jake, and we both agreed that I shouldn't be embarrassed. It wasn't porn. It was visceral sexual expression, like what Henry Miller does. Getting published online made me even more serious about being a writer, which meant being bold and not giving a fuck what anyone thinks of my art. (Even my English professor was impressed with my boldness.) I deserve to be recognized for my talent and hard work, I thought. So I let the website use my real name.

This was the first time that someone from a job mentioned my story. I felt a mixture of embarrassment and pride; it was a reputable website, although the two paragraphs describing fellatio on the Wonder Wheel in Coney Island was a bit much, despite the symbolism of Fortuna's wheel changing his luck: he was better off without the girlfriend.

"Did you mention the story to Regan?"

"No, not at all. He was only interested in anything sketchy that would affect your job performance. I didn't tell anyone."

I wondered if he was telling the truth. Then I told myself to not worry because there was nothing I could do about it anyway. "Did you read it?"

"Yeah, I love short stories. I tend to read them more than novels because I don't have time for them. I thought it was really good. Nice and saucy."

"Thanks." I glanced at his face to gauge his sincerity. I knew better than to trust anyone from work. It was barely two weeks ago that Oliver made some female attorney cry during a conference call with me, Patricia, and one other analyst in his office. Her voice got weak and started cracking over the loudspeaker. She tried to cover it up by clearing her throat, but you could tell she was getting weepy. This was after Oliver repeatedly called her a "Ding-a-ling" for sending us an incorrect invoice after she was asked to fix the mistake. Oliver always kept his door wide open during conference calls, and spoke in a loud, booming voice, like some sort of sadistic hedge fund exhibitionist. When the call was over, Oliver and Patricia chuckled.

"I love the part when the guy 'accidentally' runs into his girlfriend at the hot dog joint with the prostitute after getting the blow job on the Ferris wheel. All that phallic symbolism is fantastic."

"I never thought of that before."

"I also liked the part when the girlfriend freaks out and realizes that she really does love him. You get into her head really well. She's like one of those stupid crazy bitches who doesn't know what she wants. Did something like this actually happen to you?"

"No, it's all made up. It's not based on anything."

"Do you still write?"

"Nope. It was just a hobby."

This was a sore topic that I hadn't thought of in a while. "Hobby" was the word my father used when I told him I wanted to declare English Lit as my major. (He was angry enough that I didn't declare Pre-Law right away.) When I told him about my interest in writing, he was so furious that he threatened to stop paying my tuition at Harvard and make me go to the University of Illinois, "because any idiot can get an English degree," he said.

The last time he was so livid was when I left my trumpet on the bus in the fifth grade. It was a brand new silver Yamaha that cost five hundred dollars. He said he never had the opportunity to play an instrument, and that I didn't appreciate my talent. It was the same with the writing. He ranted about the great opportunity Harvard allowed me, and how he and my mom saved and made sacrifices so that I could have the best education. "It would be absurd for you to work as a professor or an editor somewhere and end up making less money than I do as a small town lawyer!"

Eventually he convinced me that being a lawyer didn't preclude that I couldn't write, because it's good and healthy to have a hobby. I suppose I did look forward to making a lot of money someday. Is it wrong to want a large, beautiful home and not have to worry about how much every little thing costs when you raise your kids? This was how I was raised, and I wanted the same for my future family. Jake's dad, who worked as a mechanic, wouldn't even buy him Lego because he thought they were too expensive. "Look at John Grisham," my dad added. "You could be like him and take real life experience in the courtroom and spin it into stories…" Thanks a lot, John Grisham.

I suppose I always did have a knack for quick, analytical thinking. Law school was all I ever thought about in high school because of my special talent as a debater. So everything went back to normal with my father, just as the bus driver found my trumpet the next day and returned it to me. I could never do anything that left my dad too angry with me. But this is the plight of the only child— there's always pressure to be the sun my parents revolve around.

When I went to Oliver's hut later, we cracked up when he opened the door because of our nearly identical outfits: khaki pants with a brightly colored short-sleeved button down. "Wow. Looks like we both mastered the 'white guy on vacation' look," said Oliver.

"Maybe tomorrow we'll get matching sunburns."

"Drink?"

"Sure." Oliver poured us two scotches on the rocks.

"I found out about a good place for us to get dinner. It's just a short walk from here."

"Sounds good."

61

"But before dinner, I have a surprise treat for us."

He reached in his pocket and pulled out a little plastic baggie filled with white powder. "The last time I was here, I met this guy in the hotel bar who hooked me and Oren up with a dealer. It's this guy who caters to all the men who come here on business. He gave me a phone number, so I called him while you were napping. You've done blow before, right?"

"Yeah… but it's been a while."

I wouldn't mention the fact that my coke habit in college turned into a crack habit. It got so bad that after my sophomore year my parents had to send me to rehab. While my classmates were interning at firms in Boston and New York, I had to spend my summer at Hazelden in Minnesota. It was the darkest time in my life because it coincided with the painful realization that I had to terminate my friendship with Jake. I was afraid that if I didn't, I might jeopardize all of my hard work, and possibly my legal career. It was hard to admit that I was out of control. But eventually it made things easier; by cutting him out of my life, I removed the temptation to get fucked up. There's comfort gained in seeing things as black and white, not unlike monks who couldn't imagine questioning the Pope's authority.

As I watched Oliver dump the white powder out on a magazine and chop it up with a credit card, the first question that crossed my mind was why he felt comfortable offering me blow. We were on a business trip and we'd only known each other for a month. Despite this, my stomach instinctively churned with excitement as a Pavlovian response. This happened whenever I did blow or acid with Jake, or when we merely talked about doing these.

It had been a long time since I'd partied. I felt almost guilty for being excited. He must have sensed my ambivalence from the look on my face.

"I hope you're not offended by this," he said.

I shook my head. "Not at all. I'm just surprised. When was the last time you did it?"

"I don't know—sometime last month."

One thing I learned early on was that the quality of doing drugs depends on your state of mind. "Set and Setting" is what they say about drugs in high school health class, and it's true. You want to feel safe in your environment and be around people you trust. Right now, none of these conditions were true. Yet a part of my youthful mind surfaced and said, "Fuck it." It wasn't going to kill me.

Oliver flashed his wolf grin. "So, do you wanna do it?"

I shrugged. "Sure, why not? I'm just curious about something. Um... I was wondering why you thought I'd be game for this."

"Because of your story," he said with a smile, as if his logic was obvious. "You seem like someone who's open-minded about this kind of stuff. You wrote that great scene where the couple does lines of coke before the dinner party." He sipped his scotch slowly as I waited for some further explanation. He must have been one of those people who assumed that everything you wrote about was true: since I wrote about cocaine, that meant I did cocaine. He was right in a way—Jake and I did party a lot my first two years of college— but did this mean that if I wrote a story about a transsexual dentist, then I have empirical knowledge in this arena? "Everything you wrote was so convincing. Especially when the coked up girlfriend gets passive-aggressive in front of their friends. That is so true. I can't tell you how many women I've seen get coked up and act bitchy like that."

"I know what you mean." Actually, I didn't know about this when I wrote the story. In retrospect, the character was probably based subconsciously on Jake's mom. She wasn't a cokehead or anything like that, but she liked to drink a lot, and sometimes she'd make snide remarks to Jake's dad about how they never had any money, inferring of course that she should have married better. She grew up two hours away in St. Louis, which she thought made her more sophisticated than most people in our town. And she was a pretty woman with dyed blond hair, which provided her with a sense of superiority. It was like a bad version of *Green Acres*. One day she came home raving about how someone at the Piggly Wiggly mistook her for a British person, most likely due to the clipped, precise speech she affected to differentiate herself from the omnipresent redneck drawl. In her mind, "British" meant better. Jake felt embarrassed about her in front of me, especially since he thought my mom was perfect.

When we were sixteen, Jake's mom disappeared for three days, leaving a note stating that she needed time to think about her life. His dad handled this by quietly drinking whiskey every night until he passed out. He was a gentle, simple man who wasn't intellectually or emotionally equipped to deal with this. Jake was surprisingly calm.

He knew his mom would return because she didn't have much money. He figured she'd quickly realize that she didn't have as many choices as she thought she did.

It was gross when she came back. There was an unspoken understanding that she'd fucked some other guy as sort of a middle-aged last fling. This was one of many bad potentialities I witnessed at Jake's house—the frustration from unrealized goals is exacerbated when you're stuck in a small town. I figured there must be precise moments when a person knows that they made a wrong life decision that cannot be reversed. I hoped to never experience these moments, although something told me that everyone did.

Oliver handed me a straw. "Enjoy."

"You can go first."

"If you say so." He leaned over and did a line. I carefully examined his expression as he sat up.

"So how is it?"

"Honestly, it's pretty fucking good. I can feel the post-nasal drip already. Yeah, it's definitely good."

"Cool." I leaned over and did a line. He was right. You can tell it's good when you can feel the effects right away.

I leaned back and sipped my scotch, feeling the blow hit me even harder in a wave. I realized I wasn't hungry anymore. Oliver poured us another drink. "So, what do you think of Patricia?" he asked me.

"She's all right… definitely smart and tough. I think she has to be, since she's the only woman in the legal department. Overall, the whole company's pretty male dominated."

"I agree. She's gotta prove that she can keep up with the big boys. But there's a difference between being assertive and over-compensating for something."

Oliver was talking about Patricia's broad-shouldered swagger, loud voice, and bulldog tactics when it came to managing us lawyers. She was intimidating. On random occasions, she called me into her office and asked me questions to find out what I was learning about finance. Any answer I gave was wrong. Sometimes she slowly shook her head as I spoke, with a half-cocked grin on her face that said, "You are a complete idiot." Then, she'd answer her own question that was ninety-eight percent what I'd just said. I began to call these little meetings in her office "The Ninety-Eight Percent Paradox." At least three times I've gone home psychologically prepared to be fired the next day. It helped when Oliver told me at lunch one day that she did this to every new lawyer.

After two more lines I was flying. Hyper euphoria melted any awkwardness that existed between Oliver and me. He was a cool guy and I was the sycophant, lapping up the allure of being in the company of someone more interesting than myself, feeling the gratification of acceptance, teetering on the possibility of friendship.

Oliver slung his leg over the arm of the chair. "So, she can be pretty pathetic, huh?"

"Who?"

"Patricia."

"Pathetic? Why do you say that?" He now piqued my curiosity because I used to find her impressive. She spoke three languages and made it to senior counsel at a successful hedge fund. But her aggressiveness made me revert back to my writer's mind—I wondered why she behaves the way she does. It's odd the way intelligent people can be transparent; she's an unattractive woman who behaves in an unattractive manner. Was it that simple? The ugly girl who's ignored in high school and college buckles down in academia to succeed and treat everyone at work like shit. Maybe she was picked on as a kid, and therefore vowed to never let anyone make her feel that way again. She had Psychology 101 written all over her.

"She's pathetic because she makes her unhappiness obvious," said Oliver. "I'll bet she scares men away because of that chip on her shoulder."

The "chip" on Patricia's shoulder referred to her physicality: the wide-set beady black eyes, pasty complexion, thick nose with flaring nostrils, and shapeless paunch. Her nasal, whiney voice rose with invective whenever she cut people off in mid-sentence to make them feel dumb, which led to an incredulous guffaw. It was satisfying to hear Oliver express the guilty thoughts I'd been thinking, but couldn't say because I was still new on the job. His honesty unleashed the pent up tension I felt about dealing with her: "I think she's an ugly bitch."

Oliver laughed so hard that he almost spit out a mouthful of scotch. "Wow... so tell me what you really think, Tim."

"You know what I mean."

"I know exactly what you mean. I find her repulsive. Dude, it's almost embarrassing the way she bullies without noticing that people feel sorry for her on a certain level. She reminds me of this one time when my girlfriend and I..."

As he spoke, I realized that I felt great physically, but my mind conjured old feelings—negativity that I usually suppressed. At Harvard, there was always angst about sex— getting it, wondering if I was good-looking, feeling pissed that girls were quick to dismiss me. We were surrounded by sex and power, and I wasn't sure what I was doing wrong.

Patricia was an ugly woman, like Mandy. I wish there was a nicer way to put it, but it was true. The reason I compare the two is because of their ugly girl desperation. But Mandy was nice—she tried to please me, and she practically begged to see me again. Maybe Patricia was a nice girl too before years of disappointment corrupted her. Who knows?

I had sex with Mandy during one of the lower times in my life. It was sometime during the middle of my sophomore year, and at this point, Jake and I were going through an eight ball every weekend. Sometimes there were smaller purchases during the week; these I justified by saying I was doing it for school. This was partly true. Sometimes I flew through my reading and writing assignments with intense concentration. I even felt passion for what I was learning. (My dealer sold like crazy to law students.) Mornings were hell. I often had a runny, congested nose, which outwardly seemed like a cold. Lots of people had sniffly colds in the damp Massachusetts weather. Despite all this, I handled myself fine in class. This was where my debating experience came in handy; I was used to people trying to intimidate me, and I was trained to believe that showing fear is death.

With Mandy, it was like anger fucking, which I'd never done before. We were all flying high doing lines in this girl's room at a party. Typical stuff, really, except Mandy sort of stuck out like a sore thumb because of her frumpy looks. I was getting sick of Jake always getting a girl. So when I noticed her looking at me, I played it cool and told myself that I was going to do to her what Jake always did to girls. We went into her friend's bedroom and I made her take off her clothes. She was shy, but I acted like I was desperate to see her. This seemed to turn her on. I didn't bother to take my clothes off, or even look at her much, except to marvel at the three distinct rolls of fat on her sides. I dropped my pants to my ankles and sat on the edge of the bed where I made her go down on me for a while. Then I pulled her onto the bed and had her face the window on her hands and knees. She liked being told what to do. Perhaps it helped curtail any of her doubts about this departure from normality. It was an odd change from sexual frustration—wholly surreal in a sociopathic way. I was sort of rough, but this seemed to turn her on as well; it probably translated into lust in her hopeful mind. Her idea of sexuality was less formed than my own.

The hard part was leaving the party. I still remember the look on her face. I stood at the front door for what felt like forever waiting for Jake to find his jacket. Her little dark eyes searched my face for acknowledgment of what we just did upstairs. She wasn't dumb. She knew I'd never call her. I didn't even go through the motions of asking for a number because I wanted to forget her as soon as possible. I hated her for being pathetic, and I hated myself for being weak. I should've asked for her number just to be nice.

The worse part was when Jake made some crack about it the next day. He said with a laugh, "How'd it go at the dog park last night?" Apparently, he condoned my behavior, and he thought he was making fun of Mandy. But really he was too dense to realize he was ridiculing me. He didn't understand how frustrating it was to see him get whatever girl he wanted, which often required that he lie about being a college student, hiding the fact that he was a mechanic. He'd never made fun of me before, not that I made a habit of fucking girls I didn't want to be seen with. He immediately apologized when I told him how embarrassed and guilty I felt. Then he tried to smooth things over with flattery; he casually picked up a blue book of mine from a poli-sci class that at a big "A+" scrawled in red marker on the cover. "I can't believe how much you party, yet you always make straight A's," he said. "It must be nice being a genius." This was when I sensed that it was the beginning of the end for us.

Oliver and I walked for some time up a winding mountain road to get to the restaurant. It was a quiet, peaceful walk that allowed me to appreciate the jungle at night. When we arrived, I was surprised by how small and rickety the place looked. There was a bar with three stools, and a few tables with unmatching chairs. There were a few men in the place who drank beer and played cards. They occasionally eyed us two white men suspiciously. Oliver could tell how freaked out I was, so he ordered for us: beer, two bass in black bean sauce, rice, and plantains. I noticed one of the men looking at me, and it made me nervous. I heard knives were popular in this region.

There was some song playing on a portable radio that sounded like it was coming out in waves. I wanted to ask Oliver how he heard about this place and why we didn't just eat at the resort, but I had that uncomfortable feeling of being too high. This was understandable considering it had been years since I'd been high. But I remembered this feeling well—I preferred to be quiet because I wasn't sure if I was capable of articulating a sentence. Oliver looked kind of freaked out too, but we were keeping it together. We were a couple of druggy veterans who had learned in our teens how to remained composed around people who were sober. It was a badge of honor to party and still make straight A's in school because we could. We calmly took in our surroundings and tried to act natural, like two normal guys on vacation, not all coked up or anything. Our eyes must have looked like saucers.

When our food arrived, we still hadn't spoken one word. I took a bite of the fish and chewed slowly so as not to choke on a bone. "This is really good."

"Yeah, it is." As Oliver spoke, I noticed that he seemed to recognize someone in the room. "Excuse me a moment." He went over to the bar and chatted with a small wiry guy who kept a toothpick in his mouth as he spoke. I couldn't hear what they were saying, but the guy made a pointing motion with his chin as if he were giving directions.

Oliver returned to his seat in a good mood. "We're gonna have fun tonight."

"We're already having fun," I said with a smile.

"We're gonna have a different kind of fun." He leaned in close. "After we eat, I know of a place we can visit. It's not far from here."

"What kind of place?"

Oliver shrugged. "It's some guy's house. Don't worry—the man I was just talking to—Willie—he takes a lot of people there." He added in a quieter voice, "The guy I met in the hotel bar last year told me about it. He's a white guy from Queens who owns a factory here. He's been there plenty of times."

I looked around to make sure no one could hear me. "Are we going to a brothel?" I whispered.

"Well, sort of. It's more like some guy's house," he replied with a mouthful of plantain.

"I don't know… I've never done that before."

"All the more reason to try. How about if we just check it out? You don't have to do anything. If you're worried about catching something, I brought condoms. Or, you can just get a blowjob. That's what I'm gonna do."

"I don't know… it seems weird." It was clear that no matter what I said, Oliver had his mind made up. I was uncomfortable, but not in a frame of mind to be judgmental. I was no moral barometer—I just wanted to relax outside somewhere and think about stuff. "I'll go, but I'll just wait outside," I said.

Willie walked with us further up the mountain until we came to a small, tin-roofed house with a wooden porch. "This is it," Willie said.

"I'll wait out here," I said. Both Willie and Oliver protested, saying that I would attract too much attention. Clearly people who lived around here knew what was going on, and the sight of some random white guy sitting on the front porch made grim reality too obvious. I relented with a nod of my head, especially when Willie glared at me with disapproval.

We entered the house, which was illuminated only with oil lamps. I noticed that the wooden floor sagged in spots, although I wasn't sure if my warped state of mind made me perceive wavy floorboards. A small, round lump of a man sat on the soiled couch rolling a cigarette. He managed to force a smile towards Oliver and me. Willie spoke to him in their native language, while the man eyed us and nodded his head. I wanted to say that I wasn't interested in the women; I really just wanted to sit down, but he didn't offer us a seat. I didn't know if he understood English.

The man lit a cigarette and then called across the room behind him. We heard the creak of a door open and three girls came into the room dressed casually in t-shirts and shorts. They stood in a line facing us. Only one of them looked anywhere near legal age, not that that applied here anyway. The other two were mere girls. My mind was resistant to realizing that the young ones were involved in any way. Did they just follow their big sister into the room?

"These are his girls," Willie said to us.

"How old are they?" I asked Willie.

"Seventeen, fourteen, and eleven." I wasn't sure if Willie meant that they were his daughters. I looked at Oliver to gauge his reaction. His face was frozen in a grin as his eyes darted from one girl to the next.

The oldest girl was tall and thin, and very beautiful. She could have easily fit into New York's fashionable crowd with her sleek frame, high cheekbones, and silky black hair. Her face was a mask of defiance, as a slave might have looked standing on an auction block. She affixed her gaze straight ahead, avoiding eye contact with anyone. The middle girl had an annoyed expression, as if she wasn't as hardened as the oldest one. And the little one looked uncomfortable and frightened, but not shocked.

Oliver broke the awkward silence by asking, "Are they his daughters?" I was too freaked out to ask this myself.

Willie nodded his head.

"How much?" Oliver intoned.

"Twenty-five American dollars each," said Willie. "For one hour. You pay in advance."

Oliver removed some cash from his wallet and handed it to the girls' father, who promptly counted it. Then he brusquely commanded the girls to go back to their room. He gestured that we should follow. As Oliver started towards the room, I grabbed his arm. "You paid for all three?"

"Uh huh. Are you coming?"

"I—I think we need to talk about this."

"Don't worry about it." Oliver smiled and went into the room. I followed because I wanted to talk him out of it. I had a hundred dollar bill in my wallet that I could give him to dissuade his plan. Their dad had the money, we could leave, and everything would be fine.

The bedroom was small and sparse, with one large bed, a dresser, a chair, and a small wooden crucifix that hung on the wall. Oliver flopped down on the bed as the girls removed all of their clothing in a perfunctory fashion. They didn't look at each other or speak as they did this.

"Don't those two seem a little young, Oliver?" I sounded alien and comical, as if I were his mother admonishing him for not taking out the trash.

"So you can have the oldest one." He got her attention by tapping her arm, and stating as if he were speaking to a dog or a mentally retarded person, "YOU CAN HAVE HIM."

The girl was nude as she walked across the room and stood in front of me. She was stunning. Her looks prevented me from protesting; I couldn't believe how perfect her body was—so thin yet shapely. She had small, firm breasts, and black eyes that remained expressionless. I had the feeling that she hated all men, especially Americans.

She tugged at my belt buckle, which startled me. When I stepped to the side to regain my balance, my foot landed in a low spot. It wasn't my imagination—the floor really did sag in some areas. I lost my balance and fell down. Everyone in the room laughed.

The girls' father poked his head in the room for a moment to see what caused the big thud. When he saw that everything was all right, he shut the door and went away. I was still on the floor when I noticed that my head was spinning. Maybe I didn't eat enough food. I made a half-hearted attempt to protest when the girl proceeded to pull down my pants, but I was swayed by my dizziness, coupled with an uncomfortable erection.

When her mouth engulfed my cock, I closed my eyes and let my mind accept the situation. I told myself that she was seventeen...she was practically legal, not that it mattered here... across the ocean.

Time stood still as fragmented thoughts and emotions drifted in and out of my consciousness. I saw a hairbrush on the dresser and thought that the sisters might take turns using it. There was a teddy bear on the chair and I imagined that the little one probably still slept with it. The wooden crucifix on the wall made me wonder if the girls believed in a benevolent God. Where was their mother?

My cock was the focal point of everything—an empty existence reduced to lying on the crooked floor and getting a blowjob by a teenaged prostitute who had no choice in the matter. My thoughts were interrupted when I noticed the loud creaking noises of the bed. I looked up and saw Oliver, who was also on his back with his shorts pulled down to his ankles. I watched him moving his hips up and down, and saw what the two girls were doing to him. I had a powerful climax, pulled up my pants and remained on the floor, feeling physically and emotionally drained. The oldest girl sat in the chair and brushed her hair without looking at anyone. She then proceeded to flip through a wrinkled American fashion magazine.

I couldn't take it anymore. I rushed over to the bed and pushed the little girl off of him. She landed on the floor with thump. I didn't mean to push her so hard. In an instant, the father swung the door open and was surprised to see the little one on the floor. She wasn't hurt, but she looked afraid. In his language, he seemed to ask his oldest daughter what happened, and she replied in a flat, exhausted tone. The look on his face was chilling. He was a small man, but he exuded an unpredictable intensity. Oliver quickly pulled his pants up. It was surprising how frightening the small man could be. I thought I was having a slight heart attack when he yelled and motioned that we should leave.

As we jogged away down the mountain road, I kept glancing behind to make sure we weren't being chased by a knife-wielding dad. I heard knives were popular in this region. When we made it down to the main road that led to our hotel, I knew were safe. The rest of the walk was peaceful and calm; the sounds of the jungle soothed the noise in my head. The more I thought about those girls' lives, the more I felt sick inside. The silence was interrupted when Oliver blurted out in an annoyed voice, "Damn... I didn't even get to come."

Oliver was less talkative on the plane back to New York. At some point, as we flew over the ocean, I asked him if he felt weird about it all. He said he did a little, but that the money he gave their dad would put food on their table for a month.

It was hard to see Oliver at work and not feel paranoid about people knowing what we did. It was a ridiculous worry, considering he committed a larger transgression than I did. Also, we agreed on the plane to keep it secret.

We'd been back from our trip for a week, but I still felt awkward and depressed about everything. The trip seemed to have placed my entire life in perspective. I hadn't had sex in almost a year before the trip. And when I returned to my empty Manhattan apartment, there were no voicemails.

I was glad when Oliver came to my desk in an upbeat mood and asked me out to lunch. We went to a diner around the corner, just the two of us. We sat across from each other in a booth and ordered hamburgers and shakes.

"You still seem weirded out about our trip," he said.

I shrugged. "Maybe a little. I'm just curious... have you ever done anything like that on a business trip with anyone else from work?" I was still paranoid that he'd be lax about keeping our secret.

"Well, not on a business trip. But yeah, two summers ago, Oren and I went to Amsterdam and had a little fun." A smile crept across his face as he reminisced. "Look, I wouldn't worry about it. It was different and fun. There's a first time for everything. And there's no way I'll tell anyone."

"I'm not worried. You know what they say: what happens in Piliguet stays in Piliguet."

"You are really funny. You should start writing stories again."

"Thanks, maybe I will."

"Oh, that reminds me. I'm good friends with this girl, Bess, an editor at Doubleday. She dates this famous sculptor, Michael Larie— he has stuff in the MOMA. Have you heard of him?"

"No."

"I hadn't either until Bess introduced us. He lives in this awesome loft in Tribeca and has crazy parties. Lots of artistic and literary types go. It's a blast. He's having a party this Friday. Do you want to go?"

"Sure, that sounds like fun." It would be good to get out more and mingle with artistic types. Perhaps I would start writing again.

Part of growing up is when you've lost some element of happiness that cannot be recovered. For me, this was when Jake left and moved back to Illinois. I had forced myself to focus on my studies, while he got more and more lost in drug use. His decline was steady and complicated—there were times when I tried to help, but ended up falling back into weakness myself, which inevitably led to self-hate. But I refused to let anything interfere with getting into a good law school. Jake didn't cultivate a beacon like this to prevent him from straying. I wanted to help him, but he made no attempts to help himself, or me for that matter. He quit asking if he could read my short stories. I suggested rehab programs and I lent him money, then he stole from me, which made it clear that it was over. The last I heard, he ran his dad's mechanic shop and got married to some girl from a neighboring town.

I felt myself entering a new stage in life. Maybe I'd start enjoying life again. I liked how Oliver wasn't neurotic and self-conscious. And maybe he could get us some blow for the party.

Linwood, Illinois

Jake's parents picked him up at the airport in St. Louis, which was the closest one to Linwood, Illinois. When he saw his parents at the baggage claim, his mother, Shelly, greeted him as if he had returned from World War I. She hugged him tightly and said, "Oh Sweetie, we missed you so much. We're so glad to see you back home." She mussed his dark brown hair that flopped over his forehead. "You look so skinny!"

Bill, his father, gave him a quick hug and pat on the back. "You don't have to worry about work, Son. There's always room for you at the shop." As they made their way through the parking lot, Bill said to him in a hushed voice, "You really should have called more. She worried sick about you."

"I know, I know," Jake replied. All he wanted to do was fall asleep in the back of their minivan for the two-hour ride home to Southern Illinois. He wanted to sleep for a week and not think about how he'd made his mom worry, or how he'd have to start work soon at Murdoch Automotive, his dad's business.

On the ride home, the sun was setting over the flat stretches cornfields. It was springtime, and he could smell the florid air suffused with the scent of honeysuckle and fresh cut grass through the open windows. It was the smell of home. This alleviated his sense of dread about moving back after being gone for three years. Despite his depression and disappointment in himself, he felt lucky that he could return to a beautiful place, despite the small town monotony.

His obsession with leaving home with his best friend, Timmy, was still very clear in his mind. Towards the end of high school, he bragged in subtle ways about leaving for Boston; he liked to let people know his plans. It made him feel like he was doing something with his life, like he was better than everyone else—even those who stayed behind to go to Southern Illinois University. Looking back, he realized how foolish he was to feel superior even though he had no college plans. His only focus was on leaving—that's all he had to do to feel optimistic. It was pathetic, he thought, to invest so much happiness in so little. It was the tragic flaw engendered by Midwestern isolation: simply leaving feels good enough. "Good enough" was no longer good enough.

Jake's false sense of superiority soon faded in Cambridge. He and Timmy would go out and surround themselves with kids who were smarter, richer, and more confident. It was impressive that Timmy assimilated into that environment, at least academically.

Now that Jake was home, he planned to enroll at Southern Illinois University and figure something out. He'd be a few years behind most people, but he didn't want to work as a mechanic for the rest of his life.

Jake was installing a new carburetor when an old buddy, Shawn, walked in. They ran in the same circle of friends in high school—the redneck crowd Timmy wasn't a part of. He liked Shawn well enough, despite his cloying rowdiness. If everyone was doing a beer bong, then Shawn had to do more than everyone else. Then he would do a shot, and top it off with a big hit of weed that would throw him over the edge. It became a form of entertainment to see how fucked up he'd get—but even in high school it got old. Jake thought he wouldn't have to deal with people like Shawn again. The last thing he wanted to do was run into people from high school.

"Jake! I didn't know you lived here. I thought you were in Boston."

"I was. I just got back. What's new?"

"Oh, you know how it is. Nothin' ever changes here. Is Timmy still out there?"

"Yep."

"Cool, how's he doing? Doesn't he go to Harvard or somethin'?"

"Yeah, he's still there. He's pre-law."

"That's cool... he was always smart. So, what are you doing here? Are you back for good?"

This was exactly what Jake dreaded. He was popular in high school, so people would wonder what he was doing; it was normal to compare yourself to people you used to admire. Some might even be pleased with his fall from grace. He figured he might as well get used to running into people, so he told the truth. "I'm probably gonna start college here soon."

"Yeah, I thought about going to college, but I got this great job doin' construction, so, that's what I'm doin'. Katie and I got married last year and now we have a little one on the way." Getting married and having kids in your early twenties was the norm in Linwood.

"That's cool. Congratulations." He found it comical that Shawn was about to become a father; he vividly remembered Shawn vomiting out the window of his truck after one too many shots of Southern Comfort. Perhaps their own fathers were as ill prepared when they decided to take on another level of responsibility. "How is Katie?"

"She's good. She's a manager at Victoria's Secret at the mall. That place is awesome. Hey—do you still talk to Amy?"

"Nope." Jake wondered if she still hated him after he gave her LSD and then broke up with her at a party. He still felt bad about that.

"She turned out to be quite the hottie," Shawn said in a creepy tone. It was the same tone they used to lust over senior girls when they were freshmen. "Didjya hear she was Homecoming Queen?"

"No. Actually I haven't talked to anyone from here in a while."

"Yeah, she definitely turns a lot of heads. Sometimes I see her at the mall. She works at Barnes & Noble."

"There's a Barnes & Noble at the mall?"

"Yep. It's new."

It had been a long time since Jake thought about Amy. Homecoming Queen... that's pretty cool, he thought. She deserves that.

"Well, I should probably get goin'," said Shawn. "I just came here to pick up Katie's Chevy. Good seeing you!"

"Yeah, good seeing you too."

"Give me a call if you wanna grab a brewski or something."

"Sure. See you around." Jake knew there was no way he'd start drinking with old high school friends. The notion depressed him.

Amy came home from work with new issues of *Vogue*, *Harper's Bazaar*, and *Interview* magazine. It was a perk being able to use her employee discount at the bookstore. She started with *Vogue*, her favorite, which she considered the "fashion Bible." She flipped through every page, studying the designs, reading the articles, and familiarizing herself with all the major designers in order to hone her own aesthetic sense. She was skilled enough to look at a dress and figure out how to cut the pattern to construct the garment. Her homecoming dress was a replication of an Azzedine Alaia evening gown that she made with gold satin. People told her that she looked like a movie star sparkling under the lights of the high school auditorium in her golden dress, and rhinestone crown atop her long, blond hair.

When her phone rang, she was surprised to answer and hear Jake's voice.

"Amy? It's me, Jake."

She paused as she considered the amount of time she spent crying, cursing his name, and missing him. It had been years since he broke up with her, right as he was about to graduate. This incident taught her that time heals all wounds; it was an overused adage, but true nevertheless. It was the phrase her friend, Henry Bright, used to keep her from going insane the night she was dumped. She was tripping on acid so hard that she thought she could control the movement of the trees behind Timmy's house. She lay down on the damp earth and stared up at the black cartoon branches outlined against a starry sky. The one thing she remembered most was hoping she would die.

"This is a surprise," she said. It was the first time she'd heard from him since he broke up with her.

"Yeah, well... I'm back in town."

"You're visiting?"

"No... I moved back."

She grinned in vindication; it felt like justice that he was back in town at the same time that she was excited about leaving for college in New York. She could hear in his voice how much it pained him; he had bragged about moving to Boston, as if it were Paris or London. It was tempting to make some sort of passive-aggressive comment, but she didn't want to be obvious.

In her estimation, Henry saved her life that night Jake broke up with her. He sat down next to her on the ground and listened calmly to her side of what happened. She called Jake a "stupid idiot" for breaking up with her in such a jackass way; he was impatient and immoral because he cared more about getting her high on acid than the possibility of hurting her feelings. He broke up with her when she was at the peak of her LSD trip—the first and only time she'd tried the drug.

Henry was livid. He thought Jake's callousness was absurd: who breaks up with a girl while she's tripping on drugs, then goes to Hardees without offering to get her anything? He flushed with anger at himself for knowing he was too weak to pick a fight with Jake. Sometimes violence seemed warranted.

He got her cleaned up by removing leaves and twigs from her hair, and brushing dirt off her dress. As he drove her home, he told her that she should rise above him. "He likes to act like he's smart by repeating the big words Timmy uses," said Henry. "I know that faith is unfashionable nowadays, but I have full faith in karma. He's not going to succeed in Cambridge—that's the intellectual hub of our country! He's riding on Timmy's coattails, and I promise you that it'll end in disaster." This was when she realized how special Henry was. It was funny, she thought, that she'd known him since the first grade, but this was the first time they'd actually had a conversation. It was also the first time she viewed him as oddly appealing. He had the gangly look of a boy who had much filling out to do. But he was tall, with dark hair like Jake's, and a surprisingly authoritative voice— a result of being on the debate team. Henry ended up altering the course of her life. Without him, she might not have sought tutoring in math and science, and she might not have studied so hard for the SAT.

Amy no longer had that nervous feeling she used to get when talking to Jake. She now felt protected by the confidence that comes from hard work and preparation. All she did was study and work, to save money for college. Sometimes she even worked double shifts on weekends. He doesn't have anything on me, she thought, bolstered by her good SAT score. It was a secret weapon that shielded her from any unpleasantness as her final days of high school lingered on.

"So, what are you doing tonight?" he asked.

"I don't have any plans."

"No plans on a Friday night?"

"Well, not to go out. I planned to work on a few patterns."

"Patterns?"

"Sewing. I'm trying to replicate some designs from my *History of Fashion* book." As of late, she was obsessed with a certain medieval sleeve that she thought could be incorporated into a cocktail dress.

"You're still into fashion?"

She didn't appreciate the condescending tone of his voice. "Yes, actually I plan to study design in New York."

"Really. That's interesting."

"Yeah, I applied to three colleges in Manhattan. Mr. Lester thinks I have a good shot of getting in." Lester was the guidance counselor who was instrumental in helping Timmy get into Harvard.

"Well, if you're not too busy, would you be into hanging out tonight?"

"Sure, why not?" Her curiosity compelled her to see him. Plus, she knew he'd be blown away by her looks. It wasn't a belief rooted in snobbery; it was a plain observation. Her body had developed into the prime measurements of 35, 24, 35—an impressive hourglass form that her dressmaker's dummy remained adjusted to. When her hands grazed the dummy's body while constructing a garment, she gained insight into what men imagined when they thought about her. She glanced in her closet and decided on a low cut black sundress with spaghetti straps. Maybe he'll apologize, she thought.

"Cool. I'll pick you up at eight."

"No, actually I'll pick you up. My mom still doesn't like you."

"Okay... that's cool." He was surprised to hear the truth spoken so bluntly. She didn't used to express herself this way. But he knew better than to pursue the topic, especially after what he'd done to her.

Amy and Jake went to a new café in Linwood and ordered cappuccinos. "I can't believe there's a coffee shop here," said Jake. He took in his surroundings and found it funny to see rednecks in flannels mixed with Goths, hippie types, and normal looking people, all sitting around drinking coffee, reading, playing checkers, while John Coltrane played over the speakers. He didn't recall there being so many Goth kids when he was in high school.

"It's not as civilized as you might think. I heard a fight broke out here last weekend. Much latte was spilled."

In an exaggerated southern drawl, Jake said, "If you start a fight in a coffee shop, you just might be a redneck."

When she laughed, he caught a glimpse of the old Amy—the fifteen-year-old who hung on his every word, laughed at his jokes, and worried all the time about what he thought of her. "What else has changed around here?"

"Well, there's a Barnes & Noble at the mall, where I work by the way, so now there are more books for the fundamentalists to burn."

"You've changed a lot," he said.

"Like how?"

He didn't want to state his observation that her tits and ass had filled out, and she looked like she could model for *Playboy*. Shawn was right about her being a hottie. "You seem more grown up. And even more beautiful."

"It's the makeup." She smiled with a knowing look. Of course she knew how attractive she was. Otherwise, people wouldn't react so strongly to her at school. People liked and disliked her with equal fervor. If I were plain, she thought, then no one would care.

"I ran into Shawn today. He told me that you were Homecoming Queen. You must have all the guys eating out of the palm of your hand."

"That's right. Now I can have my pick of the football players."

He sensed the same distain that he and Timmy had when they were seniors. It was a feeling that the town was painfully boring, everything about high school was banal, and the people who took the social stratification of high school seriously were pathetic.

"So, what's this about New York?"

"I applied to three schools: Hunter College, FIT, which is the Fashion Institute of Technology, and Parsons. I'm really excited. I worked hard on my applications, and I should find out any day now if I got in somewhere."

"So, you're gonna study to be a designer?"

"That's the plan."

Jake always found her interest in fashion design a little shallow. Of all the things to get a degree in... it just seemed strange to him. But he wasn't surprised; he never found her particularly bright.

"What if you don't get in?"

"I'm sure I'll get in somewhere." She knew he'd make some negative comment. He loved to play the devil's advocate, as if arguing in itself made him seem analytical and more intelligent. What he didn't know was that she spent a lot of time in the coffee shop studying. When he was a senior, all he did was cut class and smoke pot.

"I don't think I'm very smart."

"Why do you say that?" asked Henry.

81

Amy shrugged, dreading her upcoming report card. "I don't make good grades like you do. It doesn't come naturally."

"It doesn't come naturally for lots of people. The key to being a good student is being organized, and staying on top of things. Frankly, I think the notion of "smart" is overrated. You can be highly intelligent, but it means nothing if you do nothing with it. A lot of smart people are smug assholes, too. You see this a lot at debating tournaments. The most important thing is hard work. You know what? Sometimes I study three or four hours a night. If I focus on what I'm doing, everything else just fades away."

"You do?" She had never studied for an hour straight in her entire life.

"If you want, I can help you."

Even though Henry was alive and well and lived only two blocks from the cafe, she imagined his presence at her side, like Obi-Wan Kenobi, giving her strength to battle negativity. He once told her that if people wanted to condescend to her, that was their problem, not hers. "People who are truly superior don't have to condescend," he said.

Changing the subject, Jake asked, "Are you dating anyone now?"

She wondered if he was hinting at wanting to date her again, which was a laughable concept, not to mention the fact that he didn't look as good as he used to. He was too skinny and pale, with dark shadows under his eyes. His muscles had become slack, and the youthful glow in his face was gone even though he was only twenty-one. She thought about mentioning Henry, just to spark his curiosity. But that would be awkward because then she'd have to talk about him behind his back. Her time with Henry was private. She was sensitive to whatever nervous breakdown he had; he didn't handle his mom dying of cancer very well at all. Sometimes, when they studied together, he seemed overly cheerful and attentive to her questions, like a forced Pygmalion via distraction. The irony was that during these moments, when Henry made it his mission to help her academically, he was probably deeply mired in mental instability. It was strange, she thought, the way he transformed his dining room into a classroom, complete with a large dry erase board he used for algebra equations. He also briefed her on the topics he covered on the debate team. Sometimes she felt like a sounding board, but if it was helpful for him to articulate his arguments, then it was okay to her. (All the critical dialogue probably helped her.) While all this occurred, his ninety-year-old deaf grandmother silently rocked in her rocking chair, knitting in the next room.

"I'm single. Why?"

"Just curious. With your looks, you could have anyone you want."

"Yes, you mentioned something along those lines earlier. Actually, I just want to leave for New York. I don't want any attachments."

"I know how you feel."

With this, the invective began. There was something smug about his demeanor that she didn't like. She remembered this feeling well—waiting to hear him pontificate or brag. But the difference now was that she wouldn't just let him rant as she quietly agreed with him. Was he ever going to apologize?

"So, what did you do in Boston?"

For a split second, he considered lying, but he was too tired. Plus he had no idea who Timmy might have spoken to about him. "I was a mechanic."

"Didn't you think about going to college?"

"No, I didn't feel like it. But I'm starting here soon."

"Oh… that's interesting. What are you going to major in?"

"I don't know for sure. But I want to get a degree in something useful."

"Like what? It's funny—when we went out, you never talked about what you're interested in." She leaned forward in a Larry King-like fashion, coaxing him to expound upon his talents that he used to be so proud of.

"I don't know. Maybe accounting. They can get jobs anywhere."

Amy wanted to laugh out loud. Accounting may be useful, but she remembered that Timmy did most of his math homework. *I know he's hinting that fashion design is useless,* she thought, *but at least I'm passionate and good at what I do.* He sounded like her mom, who also thought that fashion was a waste of time.

"Why do you have to go all the way to New York City to study fashion?"

"It's the fashion capital of the world, Mom. It's the world capital."

"Don't you think you'll be lonely there all by yourself?"

"I'll be surrounded by a million people. How could I get lonely? Besides, I'll make friends at school."

"But what if you don't find a job? How 'bout being a nurse or a teacher—you know, something practical?"

"Mom, there are plenty of jobs in fashion." She didn't want to say that she wanted to be around sophisticated people, and not end up like her. Anything but that.

"What's Timmy majoring in?"

"He's pre-law."

"That's not surprising. I remember he used to talk about being a lawyer, like his dad. I'll bet he fits right in with all those smart, ambitious people over there."

He tried not to think about how much he missed Timmy. It was still too much to take in, coupled with the shock of being back. Sometimes it took over a week for his mental state and nasal passages to go back to normal after partying hard. It was like a low-grade depression, making it difficult to motivate beyond eating and watching TV. And he constantly had to blow his nose, causing it to bleed a little sometimes. His dad sounded suspicious when he said, "I don't remember you having allergies so bad."

The nasal irritation was why he started burning the cocaine down so they could smoke crack. All you had to do was put it in a spoon and hold it over a flame with a little bit of baking soda and water, leaving a little chunk that supposedly had less impurities, according to a website he consulted. The high didn't last as long, but when it hit you—especially that first big hit—it was immediate, and better than sex. Jake felt like he could literally feel parts of his brain tingling with pleasure. When he introduced this to Timmy, he couldn't believe they hadn't been doing this all along.

Jake felt terrible when Timmy developed bronchitis after smoking crack. It might not have been the crack that caused it, but Timmy was convinced it was. He was in bed coughing hard into his hands, which he followed by checking his palms. When Jake asked why he kept doing that, he said he was making sure no blood came up. He could be real dramatic like that, Jake thought. Timmy said that he sympathized with people from the nineteenth century who died from consumption. At first, Jake thought he said "constipation," and failed to see the connection between this and coughing.

"I had to miss two classes this week. Now I might get a B in Economics. That's total bullshit."

"Dude, it's only a B. I'll bet you're getting A's in everything else."

"That's not the point! My grades are very important to me. If I don't get into a good law school, then I'm wasting my time here." Timmy's entire body shuddered as he coughed hard into both hands. He took a sip of water and continued, "I need to stop doing everything. This is getting ridiculous."

Jake could hear Timmy wheezing from across the room. "It might not have been the crack. You do have—"

"I know, I have a history of asthma, so that makes me more susceptible to getting bronchitis. I read that online too. It also said that smoking is the main cause of bronchitis. I think logic dictates that smoking a bunch of crack will get you sick." He had another coughing fit and then checked his hands. "By the way, I know you took the money, so give it back."

Jake didn't think he'd notice. It was only a hundred dollars, which he needed to cover rent. "I'm sorry. I was gonna pay you back as soon as possible."

"That's no excuse and you know it."

"Your dad gives you money all the time. I don't get shit from my parents."

Timmy shook his head. "You always feel like you can take things from me—my drugs, my money—I used to ignore this, but now it's bullshit."

Jake wondered if everything would be different if Timmy hadn't gotten bronchitis. This was why Jake's nose hurt at the moment. On his last night before leaving, he was so depressed that he snorted two grams by himself.

"Are you okay?" Amy asked.

"I'm fine."

"You look pensive."

Pensive... she must have heard someone use that word, he thought. "Yes, I'm very pensive. I was thinking about a conversation I had with Timmy yesterday. We're thinking about taking a ski trip this winter."

"Sounds cool."

It wasn't true, but he didn't like her condescending attitude, and the way she looked bored as she watched the freaky hippies behind him set up for a poetry reading. It was obvious to him that they were irritating each other, but this didn't change the fact that he owed her an apology. It was wrong the way he broke up with her.

"So, why'd you move back?" She was now convinced that he'd never apologize, so she decided to go all out. She was sick of listening to his small talk while his idiot eyes lingered over her chest. All the pent up anger was back, and she felt disgusted by what he took from her when she was fourteen.

"I bought some things at Spencer's that might help," he said, showing her a rubber dildo and a bottle of lubrication. They couldn't do it the first few times they tried. Her body wasn't ready yet.

"I don't know. It's weird."

"Trust me. It'll make things easier. Now just lay back and relax."

They were lying on a sleeping bag in the flatbed of his truck, parked in the middle of nowhere. She looked up at the starry sky and thought it was all romantic.

"I just wanted to."

"You wanted to move back here?"

He shrugged. "Yeah, I guess."

The strained look on his face made her feel like she was winning. Henry was right about karma existing, she thought. Karma kicks ass.

"Why are you moving all the way to New York, just so you can make dresses?"

"Actually, that's not why I'm moving, but of course you'd see it that way. I'm moving to New York to get an education in one of the best cities in the world. To me, this makes more sense than moving across the country to Boston to work as a mechanic, don't you think? I intend to get a college degree and have a great time in the city. And I'll never come crawling back here."

As Amy stood to leave, she thrust her chest out while flipping her long hair over one shoulder. It was her way of commanding attention when she walked through a room. She strutted out the door in her high heels without saying goodbye to him. She could feel the attention people gave her when she dressed a certain way, and took long strides as she swayed her hips. She knew that her body and face would take her places. There was no reason why she couldn't find a wealthy man in the city and never have to come back. It was that simple. She'd work hard in the city, but she was also comforted by the insurance of her looks.

Her triumphant mood made her want to visit Henry, especially since he was so close by. It occurred to her that maybe it was fate that Jake was a jerk that night he broke up with her. Otherwise, she might not have befriended Henry. This made her miss him even more. They were friendly with each other at school, but they quit hanging out as much when things between them got too weird. She thought about walking in the direction of his house, and deciding on the way if she'd ring the doorbell.

"I'm so proud of you!" Henry gave her a hug. They were celebrating the 1200 she got on her SAT. His grandmother was asleep upstairs while they celebrated in his living room. Her eyes began to tear up. "What's wrong?"

"I'm sorry," she said, dabbing her eyes on her sleeve. "No one's ever said that to me before."

"I'm surprised. It's obvious that you're so smart." He looked bewildered. "So, your mom never tells you that you're smart?" She shook her head. He couldn't imagine not ever knowing the deep and absolute maternal love that envelops a person and makes it seem like everything in the world will be all right. It was a love that he'd lost for good, and he was glad to return the good feeling to someone else. "And you're beautiful too." Henry leaned over and kissed her.

She suspected it was his first time kissing a girl because his hands were shaky and he had a nervous look on his face. Now it was her turn to be the teacher. They reclined on the couch and he kissed her neck. When her shirt was off, he kissed and fondled her breasts. When she pulled him on top of her, he started humping her leg while holding her nipple in his mouth. This seemed to get him overly excited. When he climaxed, he whimpered and said, "Mama." Collapsing on the floor into the fetal position, he cried. She tried to comfort him, but he wouldn't speak or move. So she left him like that, lying on the floor crying.

She hated that he cried in front of her. It made her feel guilty and embarrassed. She wondered if her sex life would always be like this—a key that unlocked strange or weak impulses in men.

She decided to not visit Henry because it would be better to leave without attachments. Strangely, she felt lucky to not have many friends, and lucky that Henry made things awkward between them. She was born and raised in Linwood, yet she felt like she'd never miss the place. She doubted that she'd even miss her mom, whom she considered a failure in a way for not trying harder to shield her from the mistakes young girls make, and the things boys take from young girls. Her mom did the best she could, but Amy vowed to do better. As Henry once said, "Generations improve."

Her loneliness was comforting because it forced her to look outside of herself and consider that solitude was imposed on her for a reason. As she walked back to her car, she felt like the movie star people said she looked like when she was crowned Homecoming Queen. She saw herself as Lana Turner, waiting for her life trajectory to be altered as she entered Schwab's Drugstore.

When Jake came home, his parents were waiting up for him, as if he were still in high school, not that they did this back then. "We'd like to have a talk with you, Son," said Bill. They all sat at the kitchen table under the glaring overhanging lamp.

"You want some hot cocoa?" asked Shelly.

"No thanks, Mom."

Jake felt nervous, as if they'd found out something about him. But this wasn't possible. He wasn't stupid enough to bring anything back with him on the plane.

"Now that you've had some time to settle in, we'd like to talk to you about your plans."

"Well, I was thinking I'd work at the shop and go to college at the same time. Eventually, I'll find a cheap apartment somewhere."

"You're always welcome to stay here," said Bill.

"I know, Pop. Thanks."

"Have you given any thought to what you want to study?"

Jake took a deep breath. "I thought I might take some of the required classes and see what I like... what I'm good at. I was thinking maybe English." Reading the stories Timmy wrote made him feel like he could do the same.

"We're just so happy to hear that you're interested in school," said Shelly. "We never bothered you about it when you were in Boston because we figured you were sowing your wild oats. And we never went to college, so it was hard to say anything. But we want you to do better than us." Bill nodded in agreement. It was the first time there was acknowledgment that something in their lives—in their marriage perhaps— was wrong. Jake found this interesting, and it made him respect them more. He noticed that something about his parents was changed. His mom wore less makeup and her hair was a darker, more natural blond hue. His dad's appearance hadn't changed, but he seemed more at peace with himself. He wondered if his moving back made things better for them, as if they had a second chance to be parents again. They even offered to help pay his tuition.

Shelly added, "You can do whatever you want if you set your mind to it." Jake noted how rehearsed this sounded, which he found funny—she never said anything encouraging when he was growing up. In fact, it hurt when she consistently told him that he should be more like Timmy. He always wanted to say, "You should be more like Timmy's mom!" Because she dressed tastefully, and didn't care so much about what people thought of her. She also did everything possible to make Timmy as smart as he is. But Jake never argued with his mom. He thought it was pointless because people never really change unless they want to.

"This brings us to one issue that's been bothering us," said Bill. "About your last month's rent in Cambridge—"

"Oh, I'm sorry about that. I'll pay you back—you can take it out of my paychecks."

"Now that's not really the issue here. If you needed to borrow a little money, that's okay. But what bothered us is that your landlord had to ask us for it, since we were your guarantors. If you knew your rent was due and you were behind, I wonder why you didn't ask for it yourself. Were you that disorganized?"

"I'm sorry about that. Things got really busy at work, and I got distracted. It won't happen again." He analyzed the look on their faces as he wiped his runny nose on a napkin. They knew something about his life there was wrong, but they didn't know for sure what it was. And they never would.

"That's good to hear," said Shelly. "Well, I am beat." She stood up and stretched. "Good night, Sweetie." She kissed the top of his head.

"Good night, Son."

Jake went to bed and thought about some of the things Amy said. Her anger caught him by surprise. Even though she was harsh— especially the part about how she'd never move back home— he couldn't deny that he was impressed with her conviction. She never stood up to him when they dated.

His instinct to be angry was quelled by two things: some of what she said was warranted, and ultimately none of it mattered. They were practically strangers, and soon enough their lives would diverge when she moved away. The only thing that bothered him was a faint pang of envy. He knew she'd do better in New York than he did in Boston. It was intimidating to think about how easy it would be for her to meet men and mingle with the right people who would help her to succeed.

His thoughts settled on the college campus—the place he thought he was too good for after high school. He was glad it was comprised of nice old buildings, and in the Fall the leaves peppered the great lawn leading up to the library in shades of orange and yellow. He tried to psyche himself up about starting college three years later than most people. It would be hard to make new friends and try to do well academically for the first time in his life. As he drifted to sleep, he imagined himself in his first creative writing class. It occurred to him that the loss of Timmy as a friend, their self-destructive behavior in Boston, and his asshole behavior with Amy could be articulated through stories. I might be a fuck up, he thought, but at least I have things to write about.

A Simple White Dress

Amy felt distracted at work. Her day, which was usually spent discussing designs, making patterns, or sewing for a moderately successful designer in Soho, was occupied by looking at wedding dresses online. She also liked reading the online Weddings section from the *Times*. She critiqued the dresses, checked to see how old the brides were, and how old they looked. She was comforted by the fact that statistically, American women were marrying later in life due to their careers, and this was especially true in New York. This made her feel better because she was thirty-four—one year before she could no longer think of herself as being in her early thirties. No one ever thinks they'll grow up to be neurotic about marriage and babies. It just happens.

The previous weekend, Amy and her boyfriend, Ben, attended the wedding of his best friend, William. It was a beautiful Upper East Side ceremony that left all of Ben's friends surprised by their need to hold back tears. William and Nancy weren't a typical couple in Ben's circle of friends. Like Ben, William was a good-looking trust fund guy—someone who was raised with the best of everything. Nancy was well educated and professional, but she was quite fat, and not what most people would say is attractive. Their relationship sparked lots of wondering and secret conversation about what the attraction was for William; not only was she overweight, but she was also sullen and prone to nagging. Altogether it was an awkward topic, hence the silence on the matter. In time, it seemed like a real thing, leading his friends to accept the situation, albeit riddled with confusion. There they were at the altar last weekend, standing together as a couple who defied everyone's expectations. This is what moved Amy so much at the wedding. It made her confident that even though she wasn't from Ben's upper crust world, maybe he'd marry her. After the ceremony, when the reception line was being formed, Ben pulled Amy aside and stared into her eyes without saying anything. Still teary from the ceremony, he kissed her and held her close for a long while. Amy took this emotional yet silent

91

gesture as a good sign.

At the reception, Amy told Nancy that she looked beautiful and that her dress was "absolutely gorgeous" because that's what you're supposed to say to brides. Actually, Amy didn't like her wedding dress one bit. She thought Nancy looked appalling in a dress that was made of acetate and too small for her. It had a standard design— strapless with a fitted bodice and a billowing bottom. She thought that most women, including Nancy, didn't look good in strapless gowns. A cap sleeve is more flattering, she thought, or long sleeves.

Ben didn't know this, but Amy liked to hoard bridal magazines, which she stored in her large, walk-in closet. She studied the various styles of gowns, and it astounded her that so many designers made similar looking wedding dresses. She had an idea of what type of gown she wanted, but had never seen it in its complete form in a magazine. She liked to cut out pieces of dresses from various ads—a long-sleeved satin top with a neckline embroidered with beads, a sheer three-quarter sleeve, an empire waist—all the pieces of dresses were stored in a folder that would help hone her ideas. When her time came, she would design the perfect dress for herself.

Amy thought Carolyn Bessette Kennedy's wedding dress was revolutionary. Amy admired that she ignored convention and wore a simple white dress. It was silky and hung straight down like a slip, unlike the tacky princess dresses that most women wear. A woman like Carolyn, who worked for Calvin Klein, obviously understood fashion.

After work, Amy walked to an unfamiliar part of Soho because she needed to get a birthday present for her mom at a certain antiques store. On the way there, she passed a boutique, and there it was—a white gown she might have designed for herself. She stood at the display window and stared at the mannequin, entranced by the simple white silk gown that shimmered in the light. She looked up and saw the sign: Eros Bridal Boutique. The dress looked perfect. It had long sheer sleeves, and the neckline was low and square cut, with delicate floral embroidery around the edge. The gown was fitted and cut flamenco style at the bottom. She looked at her watch. I'll be late...but Ben will understand.

She arrived in a cab at Ben's brownstone in Brooklyn Heights.

He inherited the brownstone from his wealthy grandfather who invested wisely in upper Manhattan real estate decades ago. She loved spending weekends at his place, which was peaceful and refined compared to her cramped East Village apartment. She looked forward to having brunch on Saturday mornings, and then strolling down the Promenade among the wealthy denizens of the neighborhood. She thought Brooklyn Heights was the best of both worlds—family-oriented with lots of baby carriages, and right next to Manhattan.

Ben answered the door with a troubled look on his face. "Sorry I'm late, Sweetie. I had some errands to run." She pecked his cheek without noticing his expression.

He went to the kitchen to get her some wine because it helped to calm her nerves. She sat on the couch in the living room and exhaled a sigh of complete satisfaction. She couldn't believe how amazing she looked in the dress. It was stark white and silky smooth, accentuating her curvy figure. She felt like the gown was made for her, and that maybe the timing of finding it was a good sign. The price of the gown was vexing, but it was nothing that eating frugally for a week couldn't fix.

She knew it was strange to buy a wedding gown without being engaged. But she told herself that she'd need one eventually— probably in the near future since things were going so well with Ben—so why not? If she hadn't bought the dress, it would have weighed heavily in her mind, and eventually the dress would be unavailable, causing regret. That's what usually happened with expensive things she saw in Soho shops. Of course she wouldn't tell him she bought the dress; men don't like to be pressured.

She propped her feet up on the coffee table, and shut her eyes to bask in pure happiness. She let her mind drift to a fantasy about Ben proposing to her on the beach in Barcelona. They recently talked about taking a vacation there. Then she imagined moving in, which was a notion that made her giddy. Ben's family was very wealthy, and he himself was a successful investment banker. She couldn't imagine a better husband and father, or a better place to raise a family.

Ben joined her in the living room with two glasses of red wine, irritated that she never remembered to keep her shoes off the coffee table.

"Thanks, Honey." She took the wine and noticed that he sat erect with a serious look on his face.

"Is everything all right?"

Her weekend bag and relaxed manner signaled to him that she hadn't received his messages. In a calm voice he said, "I tried calling you earlier... I wanted to talk to you about—"

"Oh, sorry. I forgot to charge my phone. Is something wrong?"

Irritated by her typical hyperactive interruption, he continued, "I want to talk about us."

At first she thought he was going to say something good, but the heaviness around his brown eyes, and his dour tone of voice suggested otherwise. Then she remembered from experience that the phrase "talk about us" was usually ominous.

"Listen... I know we've been seeing each other for a while, but I think it's better that we break up."

"Why? What are you talking about?"

"I just..." He took a deep breath. "I feel like I'm not ready to give you what you want. I know you want to get married and start a family—"

"I never said I wanted to do that right away."

"I don't want to waste your time. I feel like you deserve more." His voice was calm and rehearsed.

"Don't you think we can discuss this? I can't believe you came to this conclusion without even talking to me." She felt her grip on the situation slipping away; he sounded resolute. But this wouldn't stop her from arguing. "What do you mean by 'you deserve more'? Don't you think that's insulting? It's like that clichéd thing people always say: It's not you, it's me. If you didn't want to be with me, then you shouldn't have told me that you considered proposing in Maine."

He was afraid she'd bring this up; it was good ammunition for her. When they returned from their Maine trip three months ago, on a night when he was feeling especially amorous in bed, he told her that he thought about proposing while they were in their cozy cabin in the woods. As soon as the words escaped his mouth, he knew he'd opened a wormhole of expectation. At the time, he thought it would have been a good setting for the big question. But before the trip, he also told himself that he needed more time. He still wasn't sure about her after over two years of dating, and this troubled him. Shouldn't he know by now?

"Tell me the truth, Amy. Isn't it important to you that you get married and have kids pretty soon? You seem to mention this more than I do."

"I don't know." But she did know. She was thirty-four and she wanted her life to move in that direction.

"I'm sorry, but I still think we have different ideas about the relationship."

She knew he was right. There was nothing more to say, so she began to cry. She cursed herself for not being direct with him about marriage a long time ago, and for deluding herself in a haze of immature optimism.

Her pain transformed into hatred. She hated him for dictating her happiness. She hated the thought of starting over again at her age. "Why didn't you tell me sooner? We've been dating two and a half years! You once said we were partners, and that we had a future together. Don't you remember saying those things? Do you actually mean anything you say?" She wiped her tears with the sleeve of her shirt.

"I meant it at the time," he gently replied.

"How can you change your mind so suddenly?"

"I wouldn't say it was sudden. This is something I've been thinking about for a while. Couldn't you tell? I've been really depressed lately."

"Well, I noticed that you seemed a little down, but I thought that was normal. Everyone gets depressed."

She now felt guilty for not asking him what was wrong. Then she wondered if she was afraid to ask. It was easier to wait for him to "snap back" and hope things would go back to normal.

"Couldn't we just have some time apart? I love you, Ben. Can't we talk about what's bothering you?"

"I know you love me... and I love you. I just don't love you enough. I can't waste any more of your time."

"Is there someone else?"

"No. That's not what this is about. Listen, I just stated the reasons why I think we should break up. I feel like you're not listening. I'm not just sitting here lying to you."

"I wasn't accusing you of lying. I just want to be sure you mean what you say, because you seem flippant." She thought of the wedding, and how he kissed her afterwards. Do all men just fall out of love without discussing anything?

"If you can't trust me after two years, then we should end it now."

It's really over... I'm alone again, she thought, grabbing her bag and walking away.

"Are you okay?" he asked.

Without saying anything, she went out his front door realizing that this was the last time she'd ever set foot in his brownstone.

In the morning, Amy stayed in bed and cried as hard as she had all night. When she pictured Ben's tall, lean body, his boyish face, and wavy brown hair, she wavered between hatred and intense longing. He'd been her third boyfriend since moving to New York, and he was the only one who was unconditionally kind. She fell madly in love with her last boyfriend, Nick. But at the time, she was too naive to realize that men don't have to be distant and harsh to be interesting. This is what hurt her the most: Ben had always been fundamentally decent and kind, yet after two and a half years he dismissed her without even trying to make it work. She wondered why it lasted so long.

The phone rang. She cleared her throat and answered. "Hello?"

"It's me. I'm sorry to bother you about this, but I have a job interview on Monday and I need to pick up my suit." *His navy suit... he left it here after the wedding.* "I can't get it tomorrow because I promised William I'd help him move Nancy's stuff. If it's not a good time, it's no big deal."

"No, it's fine. You can come by."

"Will you be there when I pick it up?"

She could tell he didn't want to see her. As much as she wanted to talk to him, she thought a little distance might help. "You can come by at one. I won't be here."

"I need to return your keys. I'll leave them under the doormat."

"Sure, okay."

After they ended the call, she stared at the ceiling, immobilized by depression. She couldn't believe this was actually happening— starting over again at thirty-four. She could already see herself going out to bars with her girlfriends, like she always did when she was single. There would always be the inevitable guy with his ego bolstered by intoxication willing to buy her a drink and chat her up. She'd listen to his stories and watch him feign interest in her stories while forcing his eyes away from her breasts. As usual, she'd wonder if she was mainly viewed as a trophy. Maybe this was all right at this point in her life.

She thought about Nancy, and how lucky she was to meet someone who truly loved her. *How did a sloppy girl like her manage to accomplish this?* This made her wonder how others perceive her. Objectively, she was attractive—otherwise so many men wouldn't gawk at her. But clearly there was something wrong. She felt like Josef K. in *The Trial*—accused of an unspecified crime. Was her "crime" being in denial about her prospects? Perhaps she was fooling herself into believing she was an interesting, artistic urbanite. Over the past few years, her life in New York began to feel meaningless, and she felt meaningless to others. She wondered what happened to the ambitious girl she used to be. The one who moved to New York City by herself to get a college degree and find happiness. She thought it was preordained for someone like her to succeed. Wasn't life supposed to be easier for the highly attractive? Now it just felt like a mistake to study fashion, as it hadn't led to anything substantial. She was beginning to feel embarrassed telling people she was thirty-four, and the assistant to a designer who was best known in the Eighties.

Eventually, she mustered the effort to get dressed and leave her apartment. It was good to be forced outside, because otherwise it would be difficult to move or even eat. She planned to go to her favorite diner and try to figure out what she was doing wrong; the march of time weighed heavily in her mind... Manhattan was beginning to feel like a prison.

Ben let himself in, and called out to Amy. He was relieved that she was gone like she said she'd be, not that he was angry with her. He found her beautiful and kind, but he didn't like how she tied up her identity and happiness too much in him. All the pressure and neediness made him feel like the relationship grew inauthentic—rooted mainly in her psychological comfort. And he was sick of watching her make goo-goo eyes at the cute babies in strollers that populated his neighborhood.

He'd spent weeks reflecting on the flaws of their relationship. He realized that he was in a state of arrested development when he first met her. He was twenty-nine then, and still identified with his younger, more nerdy persona that made it difficult to date in high school and college.

He first met Amy at a party, and his initial instinct was that she would never go out with him. He usually didn't go out with women who looked like they could be a model or an actress. She reminded him of a girl he was obsessed with at Penn State. Her name was Libby, and she was a common topic of discussion in his dorm. Most of the guys (with the exception of the cavalier frat boy types) were intimidated by her looks and pedigree. She often ate dinner in the cafeteria alone, which gave her an air of mystery. Was she shunned by other girls? Did she have any real friends?

On a night when Ben was feeling particularly bold, he decided to talk to Libby in the cafeteria. His main concern was that she was probably sick of guys hitting on her all the time. But would he be hitting on her? Is talking to a fellow classmate something to be frowned upon? So he decided to approach her, feeling protected by his introversion; shame exists in relation to other people, so he conjectured that no one would find out if she shot him down if no one was around to see. It was worth a try.

He approached her carrying his tray of food, prepared to introduce himself, and maybe bring up the history class they had together last semester. When he got to her table, she set down her book and glanced up at him with a quizzical look. He opened his mouth, but nothing came out. Not a sound. He still remembered the blueness of her eyes, and the way her dark eyebrows knitted in confusion over why he just stood there with his mouth open in a precursor to speech. Before it became too apparent that he was an impossible misfit, he walked away, hoping no one noticed his failure.

When Ben first met Amy, he was struck by her physical similarity to Libby, except she was even more striking. Amy was taller, more filled-out, and her blond wavy hair was thicker and fuller of life. Even her eyes were bluer. When he went over to introduce himself to her, she smiled and said hello first. They were at a party hosted by a mutual friend, so they automatically had something to talk about. She was drunk and friendly, lightly touching his arm when she spoke. Her voice had a non-pretentious Midwestern twang.

Ben came to the conclusion that Amy's good looks masked

warning signals that he overlooked and forgot about until recently. The thing with being a nerd, he realized, is that any semblance of affection from a pretty girl is blown out of proportion, and all sins are forgiven. For example, he should have known something was wrong when she talked a little too much about her past success. He chalked this up to a certain "small town Midwesterness" that grew more apparent as their relationship progressed. He suspected that back home she was a big fish in a small pond, but here her lack of success in the fashion industry weighed down her ego. Her coping mechanism, he decided, was to mention past achievements, like being crowned Homecoming Queen and posing in a beer ad for some microbrewery when she was twenty-one. As time progressed, she focused on getting married. He felt like it was just as important to her to be married, as it was to be married to him.

He looked around her apartment and felt annoyed that she didn't think to place his suit anywhere visible. This wasn't surprising considering she was prone to distraction. Maneuvering around empty bags of junk food, magazines, sketches, and clothes, he made his way across her bedroom to the walk-in closet. He switched on the light to discover that the floor was covered with shoes and dirty laundry, and the closet was so packed with clothes that he didn't know where to begin. He never understood her obsession with shopping, and her dream of having her own line of clothing embarrassed him. He didn't want to spend the rest of his life talking about clothes and shoes.

In a way, he felt sorry for people like her from little Midwestern towns in the middle of nowhere. He discussed this with William last night, and he came to the conclusion that they're disadvantaged and unprepared for New York when they come here. They put "New York City" up on a pedestal, as if just being here is good enough to feel better than everyone else back home, even if you don't succeed.

He looked around and saw three garment bags at the back of the closet. Stepping over the mess, he unzipped one of them. Relieved that he found his suit, he then noticed that the garment bag next to it said: "Eros Bridal Boutique." He unzipped it and saw a long-sleeved white gown. The receipt attached to the hanger revealed that it was purchased yesterday. Amy had obsessed over how ugly Nancy's strapless wedding dress was, and how she would wear a long-sleeved wedding gown. He felt nervous all of a sudden as he carefully zipped up the bag. His instinct was to flee, but before leaving, his curiosity made him look in the other garment bag. It was another wedding gown, and this one looked like Nancy's—strapless and puffy like a princess dress. The receipt attached to the hanger revealed that it was from a bridal salon on the Upper East Side. The date read: December 12, 2001. She was dating Nick at the time.

Now he was really nervous. He turned to leave, but almost tripped over a plastic crate. He looked down and saw that it overflowed with bridal magazines. He then noticed two boxes filled with these magazines, each one featuring a glowing bride on the cover, ecstatic as if she'd just won an Oscar. He now knew that he was escaping something larger than he realized.

He swiftly left the apartment, leaving the key under the doormat. He walked away briskly with his suit slung over his shoulder. After a few blocks, he began to jog. Instead of taking the subway home, he then hailed a cab and got in to avoid detection.

From Out of Nowhere

After settling in at his hotel in Union Square, Jake Murdoch showered, put on fresh clothes, and stepped out into the bright sunshine and bustling sidewalks. He was intimidated, but invigorated by his surroundings. It seemed like the best possible time of year to visit New York; he'd never seen so many gorgeous women walking around in their little spring dresses. He noticed that men gawked at them openly, as if this was part of New York culture—appreciating the walking art forms that surrounded them.

Seeing how hot the women were reminded him of a not so distant past when he lived in Boston with his friend, Timmy. He liked to exploit his talents at seducing college girls, most of whom looked past the fact that he wasn't in college himself. He excelled at getting laid where Timmy excelled in academia. Sometimes Timmy was envious, but never uncool about it. He probably knew that going to Harvard would pay off more in the long run in terms of life happiness.

Jake sipped an iced coffee at an outdoor café and people watched as he killed time before meeting his agent. He loved the way people walked quickly as if everyone had something important to do. And it was a Saturday afternoon, creating an added energy about weekend fun.

Looking around him, it felt funny that he'd been in small town Linwood, Illinois just that morning. He never thought his greatest life achievement would be shaped in Southern Illinois—sitting at his mundane office job between making copies for professors and filing documents. After earning his bachelor's degree in English four years ago, he made a living as an Administrative Assistant in the English department. He dedicated his mental energy to writing fiction as he trudged through his days of secretarial duties that paid the bills and allowed him to write at work.

In lieu of socializing much over the past year, Jake wrote a novel, found an agent at a top Manhattan literary agency, and then got a book deal. It shouldn't have happened, he often thought, but it did. And now he was in New York to meet his agent in person for the first time, and hold the actual book in his hands. Later that evening he'd do his first reading at a bookstore café in Soho. In a month's time, he'd fly to the East coast again for his Northeastern book tour.

Riding the wave of destiny was still sinking in. He felt like he was on a spiritual journey, as if he were a spectator in something larger than himself. It was a humbling feeling that didn't come naturally to him when he was younger. Now that he was twenty-eight, he knew how important it was to work hard at something and take life seriously. This was why he insisted that his girlfriend, Jennifer, not go with him even though she wanted to badly. She would have annoyed him with her constant questions and hanging on his arm without pause. He wanted to experience New York on his own, making it a more pure experience. She protested, but eventually relented when he convinced her that he needed to focus on doing a good reading, which he could only do alone. She believed him.

Jennifer's love for him was beginning to make him question her judgment, not that he wasn't flattered. She was a highly attractive college sophomore studying to be a nurse. He met her in the English department when she came in one day to have lunch with her father, who was the Dean if the department. In other words, his boss. Jennifer constantly told Jake how handsome and funny he was, and she found his stories about living in Boston absolutely fascinating. He knew he was a good storyteller—especially when it came to talking about wild parties or funny observations he and Timmy would make—but his anecdotes probably wouldn't impress her as much if she hadn't been from a little town just like Linwood in Southern Illinois. She'd never traveled anywhere or looked beyond attending Southern Illinois University. It made sense since her dad was a dean, but Jake could tell she was one of those girls who thought about marrying every guy she dated, even back in high school.

Despite this, it was impossible to not ask her out because of her dark good looks—hair as dark brown as his, hazel eyes, olive skin, and a naturally thin, but athletic build. (It was shallow of him to think this, but she was one of the few girls on campus who was good looking enough for him.) Before he knew it, a few dates turned into a year of dating. He'd never been with anyone for a year, and it scared him; he sensed an unspoken mandate to discuss whether or not they'd marry, and he wasn't sure if he was ready for marriage yet, or if he wanted to be with her. This was another reason he didn't want her with him in New York; he needed to clear his head. His instinct told him that their relationship was tainted by her inexperience. It used to be a point of pride to attract women so easily, but the ease with which he enamored her struck him as suspect. He figured this was part of getting older; memories of past accomplishments were transformed into uninformed delusion.

Lately he'd been thinking about how he had Jennifer to thank in a way for his book. When they first started dating, he went to her apartment and noticed a bunch of chick lit books lying around. He perused them and couldn't believe that stuff like that got published. Their formulaic quality cracked him up; there was always a woman who felt victimized by men or society and had to go "find herself" to make things right. This often entailed going to an exotic locale and describing indulges into delicious food, drinks, a cast of wacky characters, and the inevitable new lover. Their one-dimensional stylistic quality convinced him that they were written to make the hordes of plain girls all over the world feel better about themselves. He also didn't like how some of these books tried too hard to be witty, especially *Bridget Jones's Diary*. When he looked through that one, he thought it was so shallow that it had to be satire. He was shocked to learn that it was not. Amused, he kept reading it, as well as some of Jennifer's other books. He eventually said to himself, fuck chick lit—I'm gonna write dick lit.

He'd written some strong short stories for creative writing classes and was trying to get a collection together, but he'd never attempted a novel. The fact that he was only halfway serious in his approach may have helped his progress; without overanalyzing anything, he interspersed humor with the naked sexual desire of two male college students at Harvard. He threw in diary entries of a young woman with much raunchier thoughts than Bridget Jones, and he made her a witch to ride the wave of interest in magic, thanks to Harry Potter. The result was *The Witch's Diary*, which his agent, Lilith Stein, said was "something nice and naughty for both men and women to enjoy." When she called him with the good news of offering representation, he thought someone was playing a joke on him until he realized no one else was aware he'd queried her. It caused a strange sensation his old friend Timmy used to describe as feeling like he was in a movie. It felt unreal, like he was being observed by an unseen entity to see what would happen next. He was so shocked that he could only halfway absorb what Lilith was saying about contracts, percentages, editing. But the gist of it had sunk in: she was the president of a top literary agency in New York, and she already knew someone who might be interested in buying his book. She told him that his timing was really good because she was just out with one of her editor friends who said he was looking for a new, younger Chuck Palahniuk.

Jake was alone in his apartment wearing only boxer shorts and socks when he got the news. After hanging up the phone, he cranked up the music and erratic dancing ensued—a perfect cinematic action for the best feeling he'd ever had in his life: a feeling of accomplishment earned.

The sleek interior of the Lilith Stein Agency was impressive with its marble floor, leather couches, sharply dressed young employees milling about, looking pleased with themselves. At one point he might have felt bitter about not being one of them—a person of privilege who's connected to the world of academia and money. Now he felt better than them. He figured their parents probably shelled out over a hundred fifty grand for their educations so they could work in a slick Manhattan office making forty grand a year. Here I am, he thought, a graduate of Podunk University, and they're working to advance my career. He laughed inside sitting in the waiting room at the agency, realizing that he'd truly compensated for the lost years of his life.

Lilith came out and greeted him. "Mr. Murdoch! What a pleasure." She shook his hand, enclosing it with both of hers.

"Please, call me Jake."

"And you may call me Lilith. We're pretty informal around here." He was glad that she was as warm and friendly as she was on the phone. He didn't expect her to be so striking since he'd gathered she was a woman in her late forties from reading about her career online. She wore a form fitting black dress and had her blondish-gray hair cut into a sharp bob. She looked like a supermodel who happened to be older. Her piercing blue eyes reminded him of his own; he knew he was in the presence of a sharp, professional charmer. His agenda was to charm her right back. Now that he'd tasted success by selling a book, he'd want to sell another.

They went to her office where they were greeted by a man and a cute blond woman who could have passed for her daughter. They all held up little plastic cups filled with champagne. "Congratulations!" they said in unison with huge smiles on their faces. The young woman, who had a "sexy librarian" look with her horn-rimmed frames, handed him a cup of champagne. "We've all been very anxious to meet you," said Lilith. "Please, have a seat. This is Andy, he's an agent here in the non-fiction division, and this is Kat, your editor, whom I'm sure you're well acquainted with by now."

"It's so nice to finally meet you in person," said Kat. She exuded the same warmth Lilith did with her kind eyes.

"It's great to meet you. I don't think I've ever emailed back and forth with anyone as much as you."

"You've been great to work with. You really have. So, what do you think?" She stepped aside and gestured behind Lilith's desk to a four-foot cardboard cutout of the book cover. It had an illustration of two men in profile peering at a beautiful blond woman in a black dress seated in the distance at a café table. The blackness of her dress contrasted with the other muted shades of brown, blue, and green. The title was in a curled forest green script.

He could feel everyone's expectant gaze boring into him, waiting for his response as his eyes lingered over the cover design. "I love it. It has a nice film noir quality."

"We thought so too," said Lilith. "And here's the real thing." Lilith handed him his book. All three hundred pages of it with the sleek cover, and his black and white author's photo on the jacket. "This is the part we love," she said. "Seeing authors hold their books for the first time."

In his effeminate lisp, Andy asked, "Mind if I snap of a photo for the company website?"

"Not at all." Jake stepped in front of Lilith's crowded bookcase and smiled broadly while holding his book.

He returned to looking at the book and shook his head. "It's unbelievable. Just amazing. Thank you so much!"

"You earned it," said Kat.

Andy said, "Well, I better get back. I just wanted to meet you. I've heard good things about our new Midwestern author!"

"Nice meeting you."

Kat shut the door and sat down in the chair next to Jake. "I hope you're as excited as we are," said Lilith. "We think your projections are going to be impressive. The publishing world likes to choose a new bad boy when the timing is right. Bret Easton Ellis, Nick Hornby, Chuck Palahniuk... this could be huge. Like we discussed, your timing was really good because of the market being flushed with chick lit. You should expect to get a lot of reviews soon. You're still clear for tomorrow?"

"Yes."

"Good. We have two interviews lined up for you. And the next day you have an interview and photo shoot. Kat will give you details before you leave. So... how do you feel?"

He shrugged and took a deep breath. "Overwhelmed, but happy."

"You should be. All the guys out there need something fun to read this summer. As soon as the publicity machine really gets rolling, we're gonna focus on that. Don't get me wrong—we don't have anything against chick lit. We represent a lot of those authors, but it's time to even out the field a bit."

Kat asked, "Are you nervous about your reading tonight?"

"I'm not gonna lie, I'm a little nervous."

"You're going to do fine. Just remember to breathe and relax, take it slow, and don't let anyone get to you."

"Get to me?"

"Oh, that's another thing we need to discuss," said Lilith. "I take it you've read some of your reviews?"

"Actually I haven't."

"That's okay, these are brand new reviews in smaller newspapers. There've been some remarks that your book is misogynistic. I'm curious, what do you have to say about that?"

"Did female reviewers say this?"

"Do you know, Kat?"

"Yes, I think it's been mainly female reviewers."

"Well, I don't care what females think... just kidding." Both women howled with laughter.

"Oh my goodness, you're funny," said Lilith. "But seriously, you might want to be prepared for this issue because there's going to be a short Q & A after your reading."

"I was afraid some people might have a knee jerk reaction like that about the book. Sometimes I wonder if reviewers even bother to read the whole book. I don't think it's misogynistic so much as it's just honest. And I don't think it's any different from some of the male bashing I've read in some chick lit books. I was perusing one the other day at Barnes and Noble called something like... I think it was *Love, Lose, Gain*. The protagonist is a woman who's angry when her boyfriend breaks up with her because he says she's too fat. So she freaks out and goes to a fat camp in North Carolina, where she loses a bunch of weight, but then realizes she was happy the way she was. In the process, there's all kinds of talk about how shallow men are, and how she has fantasies about telling her next boyfriend, well, your penis is too small. I don't know...maybe I'm wrong here."

"No, I know what you're saying," said Kat. "I've looked at that book too. There's definitely a double standard when it comes to criticizing the opposite sex. But we think you're going to come out looking pretty good, because your book's really funny. We like how you straddle realism with a bizarre world of magic. Some parts are really scary too. It's funny, scary, sexy, and magical."

"Oh, and this doesn't hurt." Lilith held up the book and pointed to his author's photo—a shot from the waist up that he paid a student photographer to take of him in front of Campus Lake. He gave only a hint of a smile, basing his expression on Chuck Pahlaniuk's author photo. He did this on purpose to project a "serious author" look. "Have you ever done any modeling?"

"No."

"That's good. People are always suspicious of models who write books."

The bookstore café was filled with attractive, hip looking people. Jake's nervousness accelerated his heart rate and sweatiness. He thought it literally felt like torture waiting to read in front of a group of strangers. There was a crowd of about forty people at the café, standing around and sitting in metal fold out chairs. They made him think of buzzards, circling overhead, waiting to pick at the new Midwestern writer who was plucked out of obscurity. Lilith Stein's angle was to pitch him as a talent "from out of nowhere." He wondered if this would backfire since people would scrutinize him more harshly. It felt like he was going on trial before a jury who'd decide if he deserved the attention. Deep down he knew he did not. He'd had some stories published in little journals, and one fairly prestigious online journal, but not in anything major. He had the audacity to try to get a book published not because he considered himself a great writer, but because so many published writers were terrible. Despite the positive pep talk from Lilith and Kat, he had to force enthusiasm to "go into battle," which was the phrase Timmy used to describe debating in high school tournaments.

He wished Timmy were there. Every now and then it felt strange and unnatural to not know where his old best friend was—the first best friend he'd ever had. Timmy wasn't at his Boston address, and no longer had the same phone number or email address.

For the first year Jake was back in Linwood, he came very close to calling Timmy's parents to get his contact information, but he was paranoid that they knew about his past drug habits. There was the possibility that Timmy didn't out him, but how could this be possible? Any sane person could see the truth; Jake was the uneducated bad influence who distracted Timmy's career at Harvard. The mechanic's son corrupted the lawyer's son. Jake made eye contact with Timmy's mom, Mrs. Landon, at the mall during the Christmas shopping glut three years ago. It was from a distance, but the contact was perceptible enough to be real, at least to him. In the split second of recognition, when he was about to smile and say hello, she looked away and walked briskly in the opposite direction. In an instant, every memory of doing coke with Timmy, every piece of bad advice or indifference to his studying became real. The Landons paid for Timmy's stint in rehab for cocaine, and they knew Jake was partly to blame. When Timmy's mom looked away, a part of him—a deep, good part from long ago—was extinguished. His only consolation was that they didn't tell his parents about the situation. He knew it was dramatic to think this, but the fact that the Landons would never care for him again felt like a part of him was dead, as if his own parents had died.

Jake took a deep breath and forced these memories out of his mind as the owner of the café walked up the small raised platform and stood behind the podium. She was a matronly, hippyish-looking woman who was well known among the New York literati for hosting readings. "Good evening, everyone. My name's May Norton, and I want to thank you all for coming out to our New Author Reading Series. As some of you already know, we have a proud tradition of introducing new authors, going back to the early Sixties.

We love love love supporting these artists, and watching them bloom into their careers. It's so exciting for us! Tonight I am very pleased to introduce Jake Murdoch. He's visiting us from Linwood, Illinois, and he'll be reading from his first novel, *The Witch's Diary*, just published by Knopf. I've read the book and I have to say, it is a unique read with a lot of interesting elements. We have copies for sale that Mr. Murdoch can sign after his reading. This is his first reading in New York, so please join me in welcoming Jake Murdoch."

The crowd applauded as Jake shook hands with May and replaced her at the podium. He took another deep breath and saw the expectant gazes before him. He was relieved to not sense any overt aggression, and to see that some of them had his book in their laps. "First off, I want to thank all of you for being here. And thanks also to my agent, my editor, and everyone else over at Knopf for all their help and support. As May just said, this is my first reading in New York, my first reading ever actually, and I'm really excited to be here. Nervous, but excited." The crowd seemed to warm to his humility. He cleared his throat and continued, "After I graduated from high school, I moved to Boston with my best friend for about three years. So, a lot of this book is based on that experience. We did a lot of partying back then, like most people do at that age. There was a lot of going out to bars and parties, trying to pick up girls. This is really what sparked the whole idea for the book—that sense of it feeling like a competition. My two main characters, Drew and Popcorn—" Scattered laughter moved across the audience. "Oh, he's called Popcorn because his real name is Orville and he can't stand that name. Um, so Popcorn and Drew are best friends who move from a small town in rural Illinois to Boston to attend Harvard. When they're in a coffee shop one day, they see a beautiful blond girl that they fixate on. They kind of gawk at her, and when she leaves, they notice that she leaves her diary behind, which of course becomes a source of fascination for them. At first it's interesting for them to read the inner thoughts of a pretty girl, who they discover is named Lucinda. There's some talk in it about being a psychology major at Emerson, some explicit things about her ex-boyfriend back in San Francisco where she's from, and other seemingly normal things. Then the diary gets increasingly strange when she writes about extreme fears she has about being attacked by invisible forces. I thought I might read one of the diary entries." He felt relieved to have held the audience's attention thus far. Now he just had to read from the book. He took a sip of water and began:

"November 2. Anger. Dread about going home for the holidays. I wish I hadn't had to go to college so far away, but you know the deal. I didn't have a choice. I'd rather spend Christmas here alone, even though it's cold as hell and everyone will be gone. Susan said I could go skiing with her family in Vermont, but I know Mom really wants me home. In a recent email she said that she's worried I'm getting depressed in the gloomy New England climate. She doesn't understand that I've sustained a level of depression for years that I've grown accustomed to.

"It's hard to believe two years have passed since the protection spell. (Mom and Dad said it was so powerful that it should last for years.) No matter what they say, I'm still freaked out about going home. The things I saw and heard in my head will never leave me for the rest of my life. Poor Susan, she doesn't get why I whimper and thrash around in my sleep. I lie and tell her I have recurring stress dreams about zombies. She wouldn't understand, nor would anyone else. I have to hold all the fear and anger inside and hide it, so no one can accuse me of being nuts. Why am I angry? Because I didn't do anything to deserve that level of primal fear. The kind that raises the hair on the back of your neck and makes you want to run outside because you're afraid you'll be killed inside. It started when every photo of me in my home was face down. Then the window locks in my bedroom unlocked on their own, the voices in my head hissed Liar! and the worse—an image in my head of my mom sitting on the kitchen floor in her nightgown with half her head blown off with a shotgun. This was the last straw for Dad—he saw the same thing in his mind, and that's when he and Mom got as scared as I was. This is what made it truly real. Who knew that an image could be projected into both of our minds? And who or what did this?

"Half the reason I'm writing all this down is to have a record of what I had to endure. It's taken me two years to be brave enough to do this—essentially describe what it feels like to have someone or something evil try to hurt or kill me. The attack, learning more about my family's history, and moving here has been such a haze and I'm just now beginning to calm down enough to write it down. The only other example that compares is Amityville, but that's been debunked. I wonder if people have ever been carted away to insane asylums after talking about these things."

When he looked up, they applauded and he could breathe again. But the hard part wasn't over. He didn't know what to expect from the Q&A session. May appeared before the crowd with a microphone and said, "Thank you very much, Mr. Murdoch. That was great. We're now opening up the floor for questions." Silence. "Anyone?" More silence.

"I have a question." It was a pale little hipster chick in a red and white polka dot dress. "I haven't read the book yet, but I was wondering why you use the term witch instead of wiccan?"

"Actually, Lucinda prefers to be called a witch. She comes from a long line of mystics who happen to frown upon wiccans as being lightweight." Some people giggled at this. He hoped he wasn't offending anyone, but he really couldn't see how anyone could take all the magic stuff seriously anyway. He originally wrote the book as satire, not that he was keen on revealing this.

"Who are your favorite writers?" This question, asked by an overweight male resembling a hobbit, was one Jake anticipated. He suspected he'd be asked this at every reading for the rest of his life, if he was lucky enough to do readings for the rest of his life. He'd carefully crafted a response to project a persona he wanted associated with his public image.

"Um, my favorite writers are Chuck Palahniuk, Michel Houllebecq, Thomas Hardy, and Philip Roth." These were bold writers who didn't shy away from the unpleasant things men do. They're realists. Actually he'd never read Palahniuk, but he thought the film version of *Fight Club* was badass.

May looked around for the next question and walked the microphone over to a sharp looking young man with spiky gelled dark hair and heavy black eyeglass frames. "I actually have a two-part question: what are your writing habits like, and do you always know how a story or book will end?"

This were other questions Jake anticipated, as he'd asked the same of a cheesy but prolific mystery writer who did a reading at the Linwood Barnes & Noble. Writers are always curious about comparing their habits and output because they're all competing—

especially the ones who haven't been published yet. Everyone wants to know how to get in the game.

"I try to write every day, but some days are harder than others. I recently came to the conclusion that I can't force myself to produce X amount of pages a day. Maybe some writers can do this, but I can't. But I find that as long as I stay in the story and work consistently, I don't get too lost. As for whether or not I know the endings, I most certainly don't, and I think this is half the fun of writing—to see where it takes me, which seems to be largely subconscious. At least this was the case with *The Witch's Diary*. I'm still pretty new to the game, so I don't know if other books I write will be outlined more thoroughly. I suspect every book will be different, but we'll see."

"We have time for one more question," said May.

"I have a question." It was a striking petite girl in the front row with black hair and pale white skin. He'd forced himself to not look at her when he was reading because he didn't want to get distracted and lose his place. Her lips were bright red and she had on a tight olive green dress that revealed her amble cleavage. "Hello, and welcome to New York. I was wondering if you could expound upon the patriarchal implications of having a powerful young woman who's a witch, looking to two young men to feel protected and safe." Her voice sounded measured and rehearsed.

Uh oh, he thought. "Wow...I didn't think of that." He said this with his winning smile, making the audience chuckle along with him. "Um, you're right in saying that Lucinda has power, but she feels out of her element in Boston. She has nothing in common with her roommate and feels estranged from people in general. So when she meets Popcorn and Drew and discovers that they're outsiders too as Midwesterners, they form a bond. But I wouldn't characterize the bond as patriarchal. It's more like they're all good friends, and at times she's too afraid to be alone." The pretty girl's eyes narrowed in suspicion as she glared at him. He was relieved when May announced that that was it for questions and told everyone where to stand in line to get a book signed. He sat at a table next to the podium, where a short line formed. He wasn't disappointed; he felt lucky that anyone even showed up for his first reading. Who were these people and why did they care?

Signing his first book felt amazing, like something every new author fantasizes about. It was for an elderly woman who said she read a review and bought it because she too is from Southern Illinois. A few girls lingered longer than necessary forcing small talk. ("So how do you like New York?"; "What are you working on now?"; "Do you have a website?"; "Were you nervous?") He recognized the spark in their eyes indicating that he had them hooked. It was exactly what Jennifer said would happen.

He was equally flattered and baffled that these people had bought his book. Lilith was right about the "publicity machine." It was doing a lot of the work for him, as opposed to many first time authors who have to do most of their own publicity. He felt chosen.

Last in line was the hot brunette in the green dress. "Hey," she said. "Could you make this out to Annabelle?" Her voice had less of an edge, and she flashed a coy smile.

"Sure. Is this for you?"

"Uh huh."

Instead of scribbling his standard, To So-and-so, Best wishes, Jake Murdoch, he wrote, "To Annabelle—a memorable questioner at my first reading." It was cheesy, but the first thing he thought of off the cuff. She read it and smiled.

"Looks like I'm the last one in line."

"Best for last."

"So, this is your first time in New York?"

"Yeah, I just flew in today. It's been a lot of fun just walking around by myself looking at things." He remembered his old trick: always establish that you're alone and available.

"That's exciting. What do you think?"

"I love it. It seems impossible to get bored here."

"That's true. I'm from the Midwest too, so I appreciate the change in scenery."

"Oh really? Where?"

"Ames, Iowa."

"Oh, I've never been there."

"There's not much to it. So, how long do you have to stay at this thing?"

"I can go whenever I want, especially since no one else wants a book signed."

"Feel like taking a walk?"

Hours later, they found themselves back at Union Square after drinking in Soho and strolling leisurely uptown. He learned that Annabelle was almost finished with law school at NYU. She made Manhattan sound like an ideal environment for studying law, particularly criminal justice. Her obvious intelligence and academic achievement made him feel a little insecure. He would've liked to have gone to a good school, although being an author obviously took the edge off the embarrassment. Artists were judged by different standards.

His mind was already made up to ask her up to his hotel room. Her tits pushing up out of her tight dress were driving him insane. He thought the night couldn't have been better. He didn't screw up at his reading, and he'd met a hot, intelligent woman who made him laugh and taught him things about the city. The energy of New York made him fantasize about living there one day.

"Mind if I make us some drinks?" she asked.

"Not at all." She peered into the mini bar. "How do vodka tonics sound? Or I could make screwdrivers."

"A screwdriver sounds good." He was lying in bed with his hands behind his head thinking about Jennifer. I'm not married, he thought. The rules don't apply if you're not married.

She kicked off her sandals and sat in bed next to him. Leaning over him, she placed both drinks on the nightstand, almost grazing his face with her breasts. He placed his hands on her hips and pulled her on top of him. She straddled his waist and kissed him tenderly. When he cupped her breasts, she felt him get hard in his pants. She handed him his drink and took a sip of hers.

"Wow that's strong," he said.

"That's how I like 'em. Wait a sec—I'll be right back." She grinned as she dismounted, letting her chest linger longer than necessary in his face. He watched her pad across the room to the bathroom, feeling like his old self. Here he was in New York for the first time with a hot NYU Law School student in his hotel room. It made him think about how intellectually boring Jennifer could be. When he showed her *Eraserhead*, one of his favorite films, she said it was "stupid how weird everyone acted." Despite Jennifer's looks, he knew he was settling with her, and now it was crystal clear that they had to break up, even if this thing with Annabelle was just a fling. Otherwise it wouldn't be so easy to do this.

Fatigue hit him as he pondered the familiar emotion he was now experiencing: it was easy to dump a girl for another one that ranked higher. Annabelle was sophisticated, stylish, and whip smart in a way that made Jennifer seem like a hick. He closed his eyes to rest them a moment and asked himself, Why do I do this? Why do I never have guilt?

His tiredness turned into dizziness and he didn't know why. He'd only had a few drinks. He barely noticed that Annabelle was straddling him again when he managed to open his eyes. "Something wrong?" she asked.

"I don't know… maybe I'm just tired from all the traveling and walking. I feel kinda out of it."

"Lift up your arms." His eyes widened in panic when he realized that he could not. "Feels like you're trapped under a ton of bricks, right?"

Fear gripped him as he tried unsuccessfully to wiggle his toes, move his fingers, lift his head. He wanted her off of him, and he wanted to ask what was going on, but he couldn't speak. His panic was fueled by the devious grin on her face.

"You don't remember me, do you?" She laughed a little. "I can tell from the look on your face that you don't. Of course I was thirty pounds heavier then. I thought your memory might have been jogged when I said I was from Ames… when I met you in Boston you said it would be great to date a nice Midwestern girl. But, I guess you're not the type of guy who remembers all his stupid pick-up lines." His eyes lingered over every detail of her face as his mind raced for any trace memories of her. There was nothing. There were so many girls, so many dark-haired beauties. His mind and body felt sluggish as fear seized him. He felt poisoned and didn't know if the effects would wear off.

Maybe I'm laying on my death bed.

"Well, let me refresh your memory. We met at a New Year's party in Somerville. You kept plying me with drinks, and when we were both soused, we ended up alone in a bedroom. We were making out and you started getting too aggressive. You had your hand up my dress and I told you to stop because you were hurting me, but you didn't stop. You just had to keep shoving your fingers into me, and you knew I was too drunk to defend myself. You covered my mouth

115

to quiet my whimpers." A slight memory drifted into his mind's eye. He pictured a party in Somerville. He felt angry when she struggled. They never struggle. There was another guy there, but he couldn't remember what transpired.

"Do you remember when that fat dork came into the room? I can see in your eyes that you do. Pretty soon you'll be remembering lots of things. That's how the spell works. So the fat guy says, 'Everything okay, Buddy?' He tried to sound concerned, but you could tell he was intrigued by the dominant, good-looking guy and the semi-passed out girl with the big tits. That's when you pulled your fingers out and said, 'She's all yours. Too much blubber for my taste.' The fat guy hesitated for a second, so you told him to come over and not be shy. You got him to kiss me. That's when I started blacking out from all the alcohol. And when I awoke, I was on the floor between the bed and the wall. My shirt was unbuttoned and I was sore down there." Jake's eyes began to water. He remembered everything. He did an evil thing and felt pathetic and lowdown about the person he was. But right now he was only afraid. It was impossible to explain, but she seemed to have power that went beyond putting something in his drink. He tried as hard as he could to move, but his body felt like stone. The more he struggled, the more frozen he felt, as if there was an invisible field around him.

"I couldn't believe it when I saw that blurb about you in the *New York Press* next to that little photo of you. How could I forget those pretty blue eyes of yours? You're like a Nazi. Speaking of your book, I read the thing, and it's not too awful for a first novel. Maybe a little hackneyed and repetitive, but very revealing—of course you're going to write a scene where two guys have sex with a witch. You know what? You're pretty good with the sex writing. But boy, do you have a lot to learn about evil. Do you want to know what evil is? It's not something specious that comes from out of nowhere with no reason for it. Evil comes from choice. You've made many choices, and tonight you're going to understand everything you've done. By tomorrow I'll be forgotten. That's the beauty of this spell. I'll just be an invisible voice in your head for the rest of your life, reminding you of the pain you've caused. You won't remember this spell, but you'll always know that there are people out there like me with the power to make dumb rednecks like you crumble if we feel like it. I studied the dark arts after my encounter with you, and let me tell you,

you have no fucking clue what a witch is." She slapped him lightly on his cheek a couple times. "Oh, Jakey, you're in for a bumpy ride." She laughed a little as she got off him and left.

The two seconds of relief he felt when the door shut behind her was transformed into panic. He still couldn't move, and he felt himself losing control over the influx of images and feelings in his mind, similar to how his brain generated fragmented thoughts right before falling asleep. He had a throbbing migraine, forcing him to shut his eyes to deal with his pounding temples. Painful emotions arose from the points of view of women he'd hurt. The images and feelings streamed into his brain as if it were being downloaded in real time.

He saw tree branches outlined by a starry sky. He felt himself lying on the damp earth, nauseated, sensing a nearby sadistic presence. Amy fell in love with him because he showed her unconditional love, then he took it all away while she was fucked up on LSD. He taught her that any love should be questioned because it can be taken away with no warning.

When he first arrived in Boston, the cherubic blond girl wanted to be his girlfriend. She called him too often. He wanted to sleep around more, so he called her and said with a laugh, "You didn't think we were actually in a relationship, did you?" She cried and started looking in the mirror more often, thinking he didn't want to be with her because she was too fat. Eating plans and exercise habits consumed her mind, with constant mirror gazing to gauge her value.

Melissa, the stunning, athletic freshman at Harvard, was open-minded and didn't mind that he was a mechanic. He never believed her, so he dumped her before she could dump him. He broke up with her over the phone. After hanging up, she cried and called him a white trash redneck.

It was one girl after another as he lay frozen in his bed. Their secret thoughts, their insecurities echoing nonstop in his head. He was reviled, loved, lusted after, thought of as evil—a learning experience for college girls who didn't know better. He was the unpleasant dose of reality that revealed how bad certain men can make you feel. One thing the girls had in common was a certain unpreparedness when it came to handling relationships, as well as their feelings about themselves. Formative years were consumed with preparing for SAT scores and perfecting their academic

117

transcripts. And now that these girls were in the adult world of college life and city life, it was apparent that a combination of factors led to their well-moneyed parents not instilling strength where it counted.

After what felt like several hours, the pain and perceptions abated, and he fell into a fitful, nightmare-filled slumber. In one of the nightmares he was with Timmy at Dairy Queen, one of the places they liked to go when they were stoned on weekends in high school. Instead of being the dominant presence who dictated where they'd go and who they'd see, Timmy was in charge. He was cold and judgmental as they ate Blizzards and drove to a debate tournament at the high school. Jake felt like his Oreo Blizzard was a last meal before being thrust onto the glaring stage of the high school auditorium. He was forced to debate Timmy on the ethics of getting girls as drunk as possible before pressuring them to have sex with him.

Jake was awakened the next morning by light tapping at the door. He assumed it was the maid as he stumbled out of bed to tell her to come back later. He felt hungover and wanted more sleep before his afternoon appointments.

When he opened the door, he was shocked to see Jennifer's expectant gaze. The look on her face didn't hide her fear that he might be angry with her. Without saying a word, he let her in and collapsed into a hug. It wasn't until he smelled the sweet scent of her hair and felt her strong, lithe body melt into him that he realized he could move. He was no longer paralyzed, and everything would go back to normal. That's when he noticed two glasses on the nightstand, one with red lipstick on the rim. He'd have to take care of these, then check the bathroom for any signs of Annabelle's presence. She'd never find out he attempted to cheat on her. The sun was shining and he had things to do in New York City with his girlfriend at his side.

His relief softened the blow of Jennifer's news, which she insisted on delivering over waffles and coffee at a diner: she was pregnant. She flew out to New York to make sure he didn't forfeit or tarnish the long life they'd have together. It was something she had to tell him in person.

Three books and a Ph.D. is all it takes to stay in Southern Illinois for the rest of your life. This was one of many thoughts Jake had as his SUV rounded the frozen bend to the Linwood Police Station. It was the second time he had to pick up his son, Timmy, at the police station. This time for being in a car accident with his friend, Sol, who was driving. The cop found meth in the pocket of Sol's pants.

The first time he picked up Timmy at the police station, it was for having pot in his car at sixteen. After the pot incident, Jennifer thought he might be better off at some expensive Catholic boarding school in St. Louis. She viewed Catholic schools as wholesome, well-controlled environments. Jake disagreed. The horrors of boarding school were a given, hence its prevalence in fiction. To him they seemed like places where the sadism of bullies went unchecked, the richer kids were treated better, priests and nuns created their own moral universe without questioning themselves, and kids easily rebelled because their parents weren't around. It was common sense. It was tiring to constantly explain and put things in context for his wife.

When Jake got to the police station, he felt a little shock seeing how drained his son's pale, splotchy face looked under the harsh florescent light of the police station. The glow and happiness of youth was gone, as if someone had taken over his son's body. Timmy's sauntering, gaunt frame and annoyed expression made Jake want to smack him in his face. This urge was quickly supplanted by shame; his son's predilection towards getting fucked up and breaking the rules was probably his fault. Hitting him wouldn't help, as it never helped him. It must be in our genes, Jake thought. He recently read in a magazine that thrill-seeking, self-destructive behavior is a genetic trait. He often lost sleep wondering how he'd erred in raising his son.

They didn't speak until they were in the car. "What happened tonight, Timmy?"

"Will you please call me Timothy."

"Fine. So what the hell happened."

"I'm not doing meth, if that's what you're going to ask."

"I didn't say anything. I'm trying to figure out what's going on!"

He sighed and said, "We were in Sol's car driving down 57 towards the lake. He wasn't speeding that much, just ten miles or so over the speed limit. A big deer jumped in front of the car and he

119

swerved. He hit an icy patch and that's how we ended up in the ditch. When the cop showed up, he gave Sol a Breathalyzer test and checked his pockets. That's when he found meth on him."

Jake knew bullshit when he heard it. "You left out a part."

"What."

"Were you guys planning on doing meth?"

"No! They tested me too. I'm not high on anything, I've never done meth, and I had no drugs on me."

"Where were you guys going?"

"To a party at Rachel Graves' house."

Jake knew he was lying about something. It irked him to think about his son smoking meth and doing who knows what else at a party, but he had no energy to argue over details that weren't relevant in the present. As for Sol—he couldn't care less. Let his deadbeat family figure it out. "Where's Sol?"

"He's waiting for his parents to bail him out."

"I don't think you guys should hang out anymore. That kid doesn't care about anything. You never used to get into trouble before you met him. Don't you have any plans after high school?"

"Of course I have plans. Look—I wasn't doing drugs and I wasn't even driving."

"No, but Sol was and who knows what he's on. He could have killed you guys tonight."

"You don't have to worry. "

"This is just outrageous that you're irritated with me. How am I supposed to feel knowing that your friend has meth in his pocket? Do you think doing meth is no big deal? You can fry your brain on that stuff."

"I've never done it! You used to do cocaine and smoke pot. What's the difference?"

Jake was afraid this day would come—when he'd have to pay for the sin of being too honest with Timothy about the two drug novels he wrote. At age thirteen, Timothy asked him why his books talked about cocaine so much. Some kids were asking him about it at school. Thinking he was being a cool, honest father, Jake told him about the mistakes he made with his best friend Timmy by partying too much in Boston. This led to a discussion on why drugs are bad, and how important it was to make good life decisions. It was infuriating to think his novels may have influenced his son's behavior. He still felt like a hack. His second book was an attempt to capitalize on his knowledge of hardcore partying, which he set in a Midwestern college town. The scant attention it garnered was mainly due to its licentiousness, which included a gang rape scene at a fraternity party. His third book was blatant swill written to attract a movie deal with Hollywood, to no avail. He was still embarrassed by *The Witch's Revenge*, the sequel to *The Witch's Diary*. It included elements of S & M in an alternate realm that Lucinda encounters accidentally when doing paranormal research.

Jake began to realize that he was too *laissez-faire* when Timothy entered high school. He was always such a happy, normal kid who loved sports and comic books. It's easy to be lackadaisical when nothing obvious shows up on the trouble radar. Jake thought he was doing enough by providing a stable, supportive life for his family, which was more than he received growing up. His salary as an English professor on the tenure track, combined with Jennifer's status as head RN at the hospital allowed them to live in the nicest neighborhood in Linwood, where all the homes were old and large, with abundant trees on every green lawn. He used to dream about living in this neighborhood when he was a kid. He was a pretty good dad. Nothing seemed out of the ordinary with Timothy—not even his adolescent sarcasm that was humorous half the time. Jake was proud of his son for seeing through other people's bullshit and for being witty, even if he didn't always make straight A's. He always viewed Timothy's "dark side" as a sign of intelligence.

Jake pulled the car over into the Piggly Wiggly parking lot. "Look. There's something I didn't tell you about my old friend Timmy, the man you were named after." When he turned to face Timothy, he was again surprised by how pale and shrunken he looked. When he was seventeen, he was muscular and bronzed. He felt panicked knowing it was no longer just pot and drinking with these kids, with occasional forays into LSD. Imagining his son smoking methamphetamine made him want to vomit.

"Remember when I took that business trip to New York last year?"

"Uh huh."

"Well, I didn't go there for business. I went there for my friend Timmy's funeral. He ODed on heroin."

"I thought you said he was a sharp, big time lawyer." Jake liked hearing concern in his son's voice for someone other than himself.

"He was. He was the smartest guy I knew. I don't think he was a junky. I think he ODed on heroin to commit suicide. He left a note."

"What did the note say?"

"It said…'There were many beautiful things in my life, but ultimately it's not enough. Somewhere along the line I got lost. I'm sorry to everyone who's hurt by this, but I want it to end.'" It was a simple and direct message that Jake memorized as soon as Mrs. Landon handed him a copy of it at the funeral. Sometimes he heard Timmy's voice in his head uttering these words as he fell asleep at night—the nineteen-year-old Timmy he knew, not the forty-five-year-old stranger he became. He wondered if he'd started a dark path in Timmy's life that led to him not coping with life. It was a lifetime ago when they raged with drugs and wildness, leading to Timmy's stint in rehab. But Jake's guilt was rooted in a suspicion that darkness is something that's injected into one's psyche, like a poison. Would Timmy be the same person if he hadn't learned early on in high school that getting fucked up is okay? Nature and nurture was a delicate dance, and Jake felt he did nothing to help.

"Why did you tell me this?"

"I don't know. I guess I just feel guilty in a way. I don't think I was the best influence on him when we were growing up." Jake began to cry. "I'd rather be dead than think I was responsible for messing up your life."

Timothy's voice cracked as he replied, "You don't have to worry about me, Dad."

The gravity of Timmy's death seeped in during the silent drive home, which was really more about how present decisions affect the future. They both anticipated Jennifer's questions and her tears. Jake thought about all the awful student stories he still had to read that night for his fiction workshop. The rest of the weekend would be spent working on his fourth novel, which he suspected might be his last under the tutelage of the Lilith Stein Agency. The challenges of writing a straight horror novel were onerous. He always wanted to create something as scary as *The Exorcist*, but it was hard to not feel like a pretentious asshole who was making a fool of himself.

If there was any time leftover on the weekend, he'd look into teaching positions at other universities. He started doing this in recent months without consulting Jennifer. He'd have to argue with her about leaving their parents, but it had to be done. The stagnation of Southern Illinois was suffocating him and corrupting his son.

Sometimes he wondered if he'd ever stop paying for the mistakes of his youth. He loved his wife and son, but sometimes it seemed that everything around him was a consequence of some mistake from the past, including the near disaster that happened this evening. It never stops, he thought. The feeling that he could ruin everything at a moment's notice.

D. A. MacQuin

Woven

It took less than a minute of Internet research for Timmy to confirm that Henry Bright, the respected artist he read about in *Time Out New York*, was the same Henry Bright he knew from back home in Illinois. The magazine reported that his opening at the American Folk Art Museum in Manhattan was taking place that night. It was his big career retrospective that would include new forty-foot quilts.

Timmy couldn't believe it. His copy of *Time Out* had been lying around his apartment for days, and he never noticed the little paragraph in the Museums section until now—a moment that he happened to crack it open during a bowel movement. When he later Googled Henry's name, he found a feature on him from last Sunday's *Times*. There he was—a photo of the tall, lanky Henry Bright he remembered from the Linwood High School Debate team, but gray-haired now and living on the Upper East Side. In the interview he talked about having a nervous breakdown as a young man, which led to a therapist suggesting that he find a hobby. He took up quilting since his mother and grandmother once quilted. He discovered that it was soothing to engage his hands and mind, which put him in a relaxed, almost meditative state. At first he didn't necessarily think anyone would see his quilts, so he stitched eccentric designs inspired solely by his interests, mostly related to sci-fi, comics, philosophy, and literature. When he was selling his quilts at the Linwood Peach Festival one year, Dr. Marsha Steverly, an art professor from St. Louis University, discovered his work and was so impressed that she got him gallery shows in Chicago. He'd caught her eye with a six by eight foot quilt that reproduced panels from Spider-Man. Dr. Steverly had never seen a more elaborate quilt, and something clicked in her brain: Henry Bright could be the art world's response to the mass produced, omnipresent Lichtenstein-like pop art that frustrated artists who worked in more traditional media. By cross-pollinating pop culture with the back-to-basics charm of quilting, Henry was transformed into an outsider artist media sensation whose quilts grew in size and complexity over the years.

124

The museum show would include career highlights such as his Philip K. Dick and Silver Age Comics series. His penchant for sci-fi and comics jettisoned his popularity into the Comicon world, but his fame went global when he did "quilt animation" for a Radiohead video—a technique he created alongside the Spanish filmmaker, Gregorio Rey. It was stunning to read about Henry's success, which unequivocally made him the most famous quilting artist in the world.

Timmy had never heard of a quilting artist. It was the sort of unexpected thing Henry would do—he knew Henry's mind was unusual when, during the first debate club meeting, he demonstrated that he had a photographic memory. As the team captain, Timmy gave everyone an article to read, and minutes later Henry relayed it verbatim, shocking everyone. Henry proved he was the best among the freshmen debaters. And when they went up against a private school in Chicago, he made crucial points supporting needle exchange programs to help them qualify for the state championship. The Linwood team was perceived as hicks—an easy little downstate team to beat. But Henry took the stage in the final round with his humble form of confidence that blew the other guy away. He made his opponent flounder and revert to moral judgments. The scenario reminded Timmy of Lincoln's famed performance at his Cooper Union address in New York—an awkward looking beanpole from the country exceeded expectations while radiating calm integrity rooted in clear facts and logic.

Timmy felt it was unfortunate that he paid no attention to the art world or MTV. Otherwise he might have known that Henry had been living in New York with his wife and daughter for four years now. It would've been a long stretch of time to have his social life possibly jogged out of stagnation via parties and introductions to interesting people. It would've been nice to have more friends in the city in recent years, particularly when his ex-girlfriend, Natalia, broke up with him. After their three-year relationship, she broke it off last year because she felt they had communication problems. Oddly, she chose to not communicate this until after she took a vacation to Paris with her girlfriends, where she ended up meeting her current husband. In less than a year she'd transformed her life into the plot of a chick lit novel.

Timmy imagined what Henry's life was like and tried to control his jealous feelings. He reminded himself that Henry deserved his success, and he wasn't unlike some of the clients at the hedge fund where he worked; Henry took on risk (by pursuing art, and not a straightforward career track) and therefore reaped the benefits of hard work, innovation, good luck, and timing. Monetary success in art was like success in business—if you don't play it safe, sometimes it can pay off.

Timmy got a little thrill walking into the museum five feet behind Bjork. She looked adorable in her plum colored cocktail dress, and nonchalant as she blended in with the crowd. He didn't expect the place to be so crowded with famous people around. He saw Roy Scheider squinting at a small quilt encased in glass. Before looking for Henry, he got himself some white wine and looked at the most prominent display in the show: a forty-foot quilt hanging from the ceiling that reproduced the Mona Lisa using bits of fabric cut into little rectangles; it was a cross between pixel art and pointillism. Like lots of people, Timmy stood close to the quilt examining the materials, then slowly stepped back to see the Mona Lisa emerge. The effect was stunning.

Timmy didn't go to art openings very often. It was a nice change in his Friday night routine, which as of late involved hanging out with Carrie, a co-worker. They had to keep their relationship secret, especially since as senior counsel he had a hand in hiring her. He was happy to have an excuse to not call her, not that he needed an excuse, but he wanted to be out doing something other than sitting at home alone watching a movie while eating a frozen Hungry Man fried chicken dinner (a Friday night indulgence), wondering if he should call her out of boredom and a desire for sex. He dreaded the inevitable conversation they'd have about what they were "doing." The question was whether or not he should bring it up first. He could already hear his rehearsed delivery: We need to talk... I think you're really great, but I don't think it's working out... It's not you, it's me... I'd like it if we remained friends, et cetera. He knew the drill because these phrases had been uttered to him consistently over the years.

Carrie was an attractive forty-seven-year-old attorney, a portrait of WASPy good intentions. She seemed normal in every way, yet he sensed something dysfunctional lurking beneath the surface that he couldn't articulate yet in good faith. There were just little things—

like the fact that most people displayed photos of family and loved ones in their offices, but she instead had several framed photos of Nicky, her gray and white miniature schnauzer. Even her monitor displayed a slide show of various shots of Nicky. She was oblivious to this being a sign of an empty life. Timmy felt like his life was empty too, but he didn't want to be obvious about it. (His office walls displayed benign Ansel Adams prints.) And then there was the fact that she was single and had never been married. He caught himself guiltily thinking this after they had sex the first time; he too was in his forties and had never been married, but it seemed worse for a woman. Overall, Carrie made him feel bad because she reminded him of himself.

He scanned the crowd for Henry, and spotted him chatting with two guys who appeared to be entrenched in extended adolescence— one of them looked too old to be dressed like a goth, and the other wore a Superman t-shirt that clung to his stomach bulge. A petite girl wearing a plaid dress with black and white striped pirate stockings walked over and asked Henry to stand in front of his Spider-Man quilt. She had the Goth guy snap a photo of her with him. Timmy noticed there were lots of these young people there. Must be the Comicon crowd, he thought. It was quite a spectacle—the kids mixing in with the New York art crowd, the jet setting beautiful people, and the press.

After the fans cleared, Timmy walked over to him and said, "Henry Bright. Linwood's finest."

Henry's jaw dropped. He was speechless for several seconds as his eyes scanned the visage of his former debate captain. "Timmy Landon! What a surprise!" He bent down to give him a big hug. Timmy was struck by how tall Henry ended up being, and how handsome, especially in his trim black pin striped suit. The awkward gangly kid that he last saw at fifteen was now six foot two with broad shoulders, and a thick mane of wavy, silver hair. It made Timmy feel bad about his own thinning crown; he was only three years older, but felt old and dumpy. "I suppose you go by Tim now?"

"Yeah, but you can call me Timmy. I feel more like a Timmy. So, I've been reading up on you. Congratulations on the show, and all your success."

"Thanks!"

"I feel like an ass—I had no idea you were in New York. I've been here for about twenty years, if you can believe that."

"I feel terrible that I didn't know you were here. The last I heard you were in Boston. You're still a lawyer?"

"Yep. I work at a hedge fund."

"I heard you stayed at Harvard for law school. That's awesome. You were the academic star of Linwood."

"Well, you're the quilting star. Seriously—you've done really well for yourself in the art world. This is all pretty amazing."

Henry slapped his arm. "That's awesome of you to say. I guess we both did pretty well for a couple of boys from Linwood. You know, life can be very strange. I stayed home a long time before I figured out my life direction. Which reminds me, too bad you weren't here a bit earlier. You just missed my wife, Maybelline, and my daughter, Samantha. They just went home." He tried not to be too preoccupied with Maybelline, who left because they'd had a fight.

"I wish I could have met them. How old is your daughter?"

"Sixteen. She's a handful. Are you married?"

"No, that hasn't happened yet. Maybe one day."

"You know, I really looked up to you in high school."

"Yeah, right."

"No, I'm serious. All my friends did. You inspired us because you straddled the nerd crowd and the popular crowd, with being friends with Jake and everything. And you raised the bar academically by getting into an Ivy League School."

"Well, I'm glad I was a role model."

"I ended up being captain of the debate team like you."

"That's not surprising. You kicked ass back then."

"Speaking of Jake, do you guys still talk?"

"No, we lost touch."

"I ran into him years ago at the EZ-Mart, but we didn't have much to say to each other. I asked him about living in Boston with you and he seemed evasive and annoyed."

"Yeah… things didn't work out so well for him there. I think he was pissed about having to move back to Linwood." Timmy regarded his old friend and smiled. "I still can't believe you've been here for four years."

"Life is strange. You know who else moved here? Amy MacIntyre. Remember her?"

"Yeah, of course. What brought her here?"

128

"In high school I helped her prepare for college, and she ended up studying fashion design at Parsons. It's strange to think she's been here since we were eighteen. I remember being so proud of her for picking up and moving to New York by herself."

"I know what you mean. To me, moving to Boston felt like going to another country. It's funny to think back on how small our world was, especially pre-Internet. So, do you guys hang out? What's she like?"

"Not so much. I looked her up of course when I first moved here four years ago, and she kinda seemed less than enthusiastic to see me. She went out to dinner with Maybelline and me, and she seemed depressed and distant. I hate to say it, but I don't think she was doing so well. She was living with some guy on the Lower East Side and bummed about having to close down a clothing boutique they owned together. Oddly enough, she eventually started blowing me off, not returning calls or emails. I wonder if she's embarrassed about something or maybe has a drug problem. It's a shame because we used to be good friends."

"That's too bad."

An attractive young woman who worked at the museum walked over to Henry. "Sorry to interrupt, Mr. Bright. The photographer from *People* is here."

"Oh, you'll have to excuse me, Timmy. *People Magazine* is here. They want to get some photos."

"That's cool. I'm gonna look around."

"Enjoy! I'll catch up with you later."

Henry smiled for the cameras and did his best to hide his concern about Maybelline. Her paranoia never ceased to amaze him, and it seemed to be getting worse. In a tear-filled plea, she took him aside and begged him to leave his show because she was worried that something terrible was going to happen, but she couldn't say what. She said the feeling was as real to her as having a fever or a toothache. It amazed him that she'd bring this up on the night of the show. The retrospective had been planned for a year, and his entire career—everything he'd worked so hard to achieve for them—was being recognized. After she left the museum in tears with Samantha, he became angry thinking about the effect her outbursts had on their daughter. But then he couldn't deny being concerned to a certain extent. He knew that Maybelline wasn't like most women. She knew

129

many years ago that something important and life changing would occur that day at the Fair when Professor Steverly discovered him. Her excitement that day was like mania.

Timmy got in line for another glass of wine. He found himself needing to take deep breaths—in through his nose, out through his mouth—because the tachycardia and nervousness had returned. The symptoms were chronic, and began when Natalia broke up with him. It disturbed him that for the first time in his life he had to seek medical help from a psychiatrist who put him on an anti-anxiety and anti-depressant regimen. He never saw himself as the type to pop pills for mental issues, but the drugs helped stave off crushing despair that trumped whatever activity he was engaged in, and began to interfere with his work. Natalia left a permanent mark on his persona by making him feel like he was left behind in the game of life. Henry's success and happiness triggered the same feelings—that he was a loser, that others clearly saw something wrong in him that he was incapable of perceiving in himself, like Typhoid Mary infecting others while remaining asymptomatic.

As he examined a quilt that had a map of Illinois on it in soft shades of blue, green, and yellow, a crowd formed in a corner of the museum with members of the press practically running over to get a shot of Henry standing with Leonard Nimoy in front of his *Star Trek* quilt. They seemed to know each other. The Comicon crowd looked like they were witnessing the second coming of Christ. Timmy couldn't help but feel another pang of jealousy because he was a huge fan of Spock—his conflicted nature and reverence for logic made him an obvious role model for a nerdy kid who wanted to be cool. Seeing him act chummy with Henry further solidified the surreal quality of the entire evening—he and Henry watched Next Gen in high school and they both agreed that classic Trek was better. This put them in the minority on the debate team, which of course led to a lengthy debate.

Timmy took his time perusing each quilt, still feeling mind boggled about rediscovering Henry on the night of his retrospective, and seeing celebrities and fans who seemed to love and respect him. The strange timing of everything felt like fate, although implicit in that notion was a reason for his life to intertwine with Henry's. After considering the possibility of fate for a millisecond, he dismissed it as bunk that simple people used to make sense of reality, not unlike ancient cultures who thought that a god communicated through thunder and lightning. He used to think that meeting Natalia was fate because she dropped her attaché case near him on a subway platform, scattering musical scores at his feet. This prompted him to help her gather them and introduce himself. When she dismissed him so quickly after three years of being together, all evidence of fate crumbled. She proved that like a thief in the night, undiscussed emotions and feelings could take it all away. He'd never again make the mistake of attributing deeper meaning to life events. It caused too much pain when events proved to be meaningless.

He looked at a quilt emblazoned with images of batons and a majorette's uniform that was dedicated to Maybelline Bright. This reminded him to ask Henry how he met his wife. These types of stories fascinated him because he didn't understand how he could live in New York for twenty years yet still feel like his life was empty. It was absurd. His mind lingered over the various people he'd spent time with over the years, and a disturbing pattern emerged: he consistently sought the company of others to jar himself out of his own boring existence. He did this with Jake in high school and college, and that led to him not making as many friends at Harvard as he should have. He felt like he'd fucked up his college years due to a penchant for hard drugs and misplaced loyalty to an old friend who did nothing with his life. Then there was Oliver, who used to work with him at the hedge fund. He thought Oliver was his buddy because they hung out a few times, but really he was just making sure that a certain ethical transgression they made on a business trip would never be revealed. After Oliver moved on to a larger hedge fund, he quit returning Timmy's calls. As for Natalia, she excited him with her youth and passion for teaching composition at Juilliard, but he knew that that relationship fizzled out because he wasn't interesting enough for her. He was a boring lawyer at a job devoid of passion and meaning. She never asked him about anything he was doing, and her interests became his own. Or maybe he wasn't good looking enough. He didn't know, and this was half the reason for his anxiety attacks.

And now there was Henry. Timmy realized that as soon as he read about Henry's success, the first thing he thought of was how his life could be improved by being introduced to exciting people he wouldn't meet otherwise. People he could keep up with monetarily, but weren't part of the staid world of business and finance. I am a pathetic leech, he admitted to himself. I never cultivated anything fun or interesting in my life. I never belonged to anything. I don't belong anywhere. There's nothing to look forward to.

Sometimes he thought about packing up and leaving New York, because making a lot of money wasn't enough to keep him there anymore. He wondered if it would be easier to meet women elsewhere. But what if it didn't work out somewhere else? The possibility was too much to bear at his age. Sometimes he wondered if he should end it all, because he was too old to start over. The thought of living another twenty years in New York the way he was living now was too depressing. It would be easy, he thought. I could get a razor blade and make the vertical slit in my arm. I'd have to cut deeply, but the pain would go away if I immediately injected myself with heroin. A cut to the right arm, an injection to the left. Because I'd be too fucked up to inject heroin and then cut. I don't know how to inject it, but how hard could it be, with all the scumbags that do it all the time. The first time was supposed to feel like fifteen orgasms. Chasing the dragon on the way out the door. If I injected enough to OD, he thought, this would further ensure that I'd accomplish the task. And no one would find me and interrupt.

Henry approached with a smile, interrupting his dark thoughts. "Hey—I saw you talking to Nimoy. How cool is that?"

"He's a super cool guy. I met him at one of his photography exhibits a few years ago. Listen, I just remembered something amazing. It's really funny that you're here. I have a surprise for you."

"Oh yeah?"

"Have you been upstairs yet?"

"No."

"Go upstairs, turn right, and walk to the corner. There's a quilt you might find interesting."

"What is it?"

"You'll see. It's one of my early ones. Okay?" His smile was infectious.

"If you say so."

"I'll catch up with you a little later—NY1 wants to get a quick interview."

"Okay, see you later."

Timmy went upstairs and saw the quilt, which was titled,

"People Who Have Changed My Life." It was composed of squares, each with someone's face and their name underneath. He saw Maybelline, his daughter Samantha, Amy MacIntyre, his mom and grandmother, Dr. Marsha Steverly, his piano teacher, their high school guidance counselor, his therapist, and some other people he didn't recognize. In the middle of the bottom row was him wearing a yellow Captain Kirk shirt. "Timmy, Debate Captain" was sewn in needlepoint below him. Next to him was a square for Jake with "Socio-path" under his face.

He sat down on a bench facing the quilt, feeling the surreal quality of looking at his own face in a quilt—an image taken from his senior yearbook photo. He thought about Amy, Jake, their guidance counselor—all people who shaped his life growing up in Linwood as well, although less directly in Amy's case. As Jake's high school girlfriend, Amy was the first in a long string of pretty girls whom he treated like shit. Timmy hated that these actions from so long ago shaped his perception of normality. He used to think Jake was lucky—a cool guy who possessed all the traits he lacked, but could obtain through imitation if he tried hard enough. He cringed thinking about how long it took for him to be a normal human being. So much wasted time, he thought, with skewed social skills and anger at women for not being exactly what I wanted. He waited for others to help him hate himself less when he should have done this on his own.

He thought Henry's quilt was a revelation, then realized the whole evening was a revelation—about the mistakes he repeated throughout his life, and to a certain extent, how real his suicidal impulses were. Most of the time they felt real, but sometimes they weren't. The only thing he knew for sure was that he grew more disconnected from humanity as time progressed, with no evidence of this changing. But when he looked at his face in the quilt, he was filled with a sense of at least being connected to Henry. It was a small feeling, but proof that he was woven into the fabric of Henry's life story.

Bystanders on Sixth Avenue said the crash was so loud and sudden that they thought it was a bomb. The car crashed into the cab Henry was in, killing everyone at the scene. Timmy didn't go a day without thinking about the final conversation they'd had about their

133

life trajectories, and about their memories of people they knew back home. And it was an unexpected delight when Henry introduced him to Leonard Nimoy. Eventually Timmy sensed the tension of all the people hovering around who wanted to speak to Henry, so he exited gracefully when the timing was right. Henry gave him another hug and made sure they exchanged phone numbers and email addresses so they could hang out soon.

Darkness fell that evening when the hunched, crazy old lady in a baggy brown dress came up to them, slurring her words and jabbing her index finger in the air at Henry. She repeated, "It's smoky and jagged, the ring around your head." She repeated this over and over, increasing her volume until security escorted her out. Her scratchy and vaguely Slavic voice would ring in Timmy's head for the rest of his life. When his mind's eye pictured the look of pure fear in her watery black eyes, he was forced to consider the possibility of a metaphysical realm to be reckoned with. Maybe human agency was a delusion.

The Notorious Leah S.

Leah closed her eyes and reclined in the back seat of the SUV as her stepfather, Danny Sullivan, drove her and her mother, Anna, upstate to Chicago. Leah put her headphones on and played Pink Floyd's *A Saucerful of Secrets*. The album had a pleasing soporific effect; the relaxed rhythms and hippie-like melodies made her drift into a deep sleep, and when she awoke five hours later, she was in the city. It was like waking up in another world, which was the peculiar thing about Illinois. The state was long, and as you drove north, there were flat views of cornfields in every direction, peppered with little towns. Then, all of a sudden you were in one of the most prominent cities in the nation—a city seeped in the history of industrial revolution. Leah thought it was funny that a lot of people from her town, Blue Bud, had never been to Chicago.

This was the third year in a row that Mr. Sullivan brought his family to the Chicago Auto Show. His passion for cars rivaled Leah and Anna's passion for shopping. It was the same routine—they checked into the McCormick Place, where the Auto Show took place, and while Mr. Sullivan explored all the new car models, Anna and Leah took a cab to the Water Tower Place, the shopping center across from the stone water tower that was the last remaining structure to survive the Great Fire. Leah had a system: she separated from her mom and took the elevator to the top floor. Then she worked her way down on the escalator, buying whatever clothes and shoes she wanted from her favorite stores. Her step-dad gave each of them a credit card and never asked to see receipts.

During the cab ride to the Water Tower, Anna asked, "So, what are you gonna buy?"

"I think I'm going to look for gowns for the prom. I know it's early, but I don't know when we're coming back here."

"Fantastic!"

Anna's general enthusiasm often disturbed Leah. Since the obvious disparity in their lifestyle with Danny Sullivan in comparison to their life with her dad was the result of dark

135

circumstances, it seemed illogical to be overly comfortable.

After Leah's father, Matthew Gold, went to prison, she and her mom considered moving to another town because they were mortified. It didn't seem possible to shake off the stigma of his heinous crimes. But that plan was soon waylaid when Anna married Mr. Sullivan. He was a successful man who owned the largest construction company in the tri-state area. His house was famous because you could see it driving up the road leading to the high school. People often remarked on its size, especially since Blue Bud was a middle to lower-middle-class town. The brick house was three stories high. It had meticulous landscaping, and a separate structure behind it that housed a pool.

Leah felt sorry for her step-dad because she figured that he made it to fifty without getting married because of his looks. She hated to think it, but she thought he looked like a pig. He was chubby with skin that had a pinkish pallor. His nose was upturned with large nostrils, and his eyes were set far apart on his round face that was topped with graying blond, tuft-like hair. He was a smart and successful man, but not attractive, which Leah felt accounted for his obsequiousness towards her and Anna that bordered on embarrassing.

When Anna married him, their lives were transformed, as if they had won the lottery. They moved into his gigantic home. He bought them whatever they wanted, (including a new red Honda SUV for Leah on her sixteenth birthday), and he gave them the opportunity to change their last name. Both Anna and Leah were so disgusted by Matthew that they no longer wanted to be Golds. Leah thought it was bad enough that her dad was in a maximum-security prison in a town not far from where they lived. She had nightmares about him escaping and trying to kill her; even though he was sentenced to death, it would take years for him to be executed. In a way, her fear was irrational because Matthew had been a good father who showed nothing but love towards her. But since his crimes were irrational and wholly unexpected, Leah knew that notions of logic and expectation no longer existed.

Leah's dad sexually assaulted and murdered her best friend, Hally. It was the night of a junior high graduation dance, when he saw her walking home. There were no signs that he'd do anything remotely close to this. The whole town was shocked by the crime, which was uncharacteristic in Blue Bud, and committed by someone born and raised in Blue Bud, no less. Murder was something that happened in big cities, not by local people that everyone knew.

Leah's therapist diagnosed her with Post Traumatic Stress Disorder. He taught her to recognize her stress triggers, and employ a number of relaxation techniques. Sometimes the deep breathing and positive visualization helped. Other times, she embraced her anger, letting it manifest in disgust for everyone around her. Being spoiled by her step-dad fueled this emotion, which segued into a belief that her unusual situation meant that a normal life was no longer possible, and that she deserved something back from the world.

Other teenagers might have experienced these feelings unconsciously and acted out, but there was an awareness particular to the mind of a girl like Leah Sullivan who had an I.Q. of 150. She was acutely aware that there was something dark inside of her that would never go away. She accepted this fundamental difference from others, and convinced herself that it made her better. She told her therapist that her dad made her life change from living in mountains to living on a flat desert plane; her vision of the world flattened out, making reality more visible.

When Leah entered high school, everyone knew who she was, and couldn't help gawking at her, not only for her beauty, but because she was a tragic beauty. She was treated like a mysterious, fragile being, and for a long while, everyone got quiet when she walked into class.

When they arrived at the Water Tower, Anna and Leah separated and decided to meet for lunch later at the Au Bon Pain. As Leah took the elevator to the top, she had a familiar excited feeling in her stomach. She liked being alone in a different place, and feeling like an adult. She liked that Chicagoans didn't speak in a redneck drawl like so many people did back home. And she loved shopping for new clothes that people at school were always impressed with. Sometimes she imagined Hally at her side, enjoying the good time with her. When Leah got her new car, she was so excited that she drove around the lake and imagined Hally in the passenger's seat, laughing and enjoying the Led Zeppelin CD blasting on the stereo. Then she began to cry because she never listened to Zeppelin with Hally—she got into them a year after Hally was gone. Leah was amazed at how

137

quickly happiness could drain away. She wondered if life would always be like this.

Leah refused to let herself act crazy, because that's what weak people do. What if she started hallucinating and actually seeing Hally? What if she started talking to Hally like some character out of a gothic novel? She felt her pulse begin to race, so she sat on a bench and repeated in her mind, She is gone and isn't coming back... she is gone and isn't coming back. After taking ten deep breaths, she went into the Benetton store.

As she browsed through a pile of brightly colored knit sweaters, she noticed an attractive middle-aged woman in a gray suit staring at her. This didn't alarm her because it was a woman looking, and not some lecherous old creep. She was used to being gawked at and admired at school, where she was the tallest girl in her class. Leah was five-foot-nine, naturally thin, with light blond hair and blue eyes. She inherited her mother's Scandinavian lightness and striking bone structure. Their beauty was a fact of life that Leah considered whenever she thought about their financial situation. She doubted that Danny Sullivan would treat them so well if they didn't look the way they did. He called them his "sweet princesses" and often told them how beautiful they were. While they were on the beach vacationing in Hawaii last summer, Anna said to her daughter, "We're so lucky." Leah looked at her mother and marveled at her lack of reflection; their present "luck" was a result of rape and murder. And it was precarious in her opinion—she wondered why her mother hadn't internalized the fact that anything could be taken away without warning. Leah felt like she was watching her mom experience a second childhood.

Since Anna married Mr. Sullivan so soon after her dad's conviction, Leah suspected that her mom cheated on her dad with him, and that maybe this explained the tension at home during the weeks leading up to the crime. Looking back, it was an abstract, hopeful time—Leah was consumed with plans for the long, hot summer spent with Hally, followed by the excitement of starting high school. At this point, she was used to her parents "fights," which consisted mainly of Anna's passive-aggressive remarks, followed by her dad's silence. She never asked her mom if she cheated because there probably wouldn't be an honest answer. She also didn't care, because ultimately it didn't matter. Danny Sullivan was basically a nice, fifty-year-old man who took care of them. He loved her mom, and as long as this was the case, then everything was easier for her. Soon enough she'd be at Northwestern, or the University of Chicago, where it would matter even less. Her step-dad offered to pay all of her tuition, but even if he didn't, she'd find a way to continue with her plans, because that's what smart people do—they figure things out.

After purchasing two sweaters, the woman in the gray suit approached Leah with a business card in her hand. "Excuse me," she said. "I was wondering if you ever thought about modeling." Leah was skeptical until she saw that the card said: "Wellington Agency." She recognized this as being a top agency from reading fashion magazines.

The Wellington Agency had another Leah—a redhead from L.A. named Leah Corso. So she became known in the agency as Leah S., the new discovery by Meli Tyler, a scout who happened to be on a mission to recruit models from middle America. Meli suspected that she'd find model-like beauty from the people descended from tall Nordic types who settled in the Midwest. She visited St. Louis and Iowa City before her final stop in Chicago on the way back to New York. Leah humbly told her friends at school, "I guess I was in the right place at the right time," as she brimmed with ambition to leave all of them behind and make it as a model in New York. I'm going to be famous, she told herself.

Leah shared a West Village apartment with another model, Nikki, a Philadelphia native with a penchant for cocaine and gossip. At twenty-two, Nikki had worked as a model in New York for four years. She felt herself growing older, and fearing that she'd never have the career she craved. All the models she knew wanted to be supermodels, but no one talked about it. In the back of Nikki's mind, her impending twenty-third birthday made her feel like maybe she should embrace her B-level status as a model, and figure out what she should do next when the party was over. Meanwhile, she wanted to make it last and last, even if it meant doing catalogue work for department stores. Anything to keep her in the game was good, until she found a wealthy man to marry. On occasion, she examined her long dark brown hair, and slim, naked body in the mirror and reminded herself that anatomy is destiny. She read that somewhere, and it just made sense, because it's only natural for a powerful man to marry a model.

"I'm going to be twenty-two for the next four years," Nikki joked to Leah as they jogged on treadmills at the gym. "You should always lie to people about your age—models are too old by the time they're twenty-five." Leah felt lucky to have met Nikki her first day at Wellington. When Nikki soon needed a roommate, the first person she thought of was that polite blond, small town girl she was introduced to by Laeticia Wellington, their agency's president.

Nikki's advice was indispensable, especially when it came to which models were bitches, and which photographers would try to grope her and act like this was normal. It was also helpful to witness firsthand how a model should eat, which was in effect, not much at all. The cocaine helped.

Leah began her New York journal with the observation that the city was a "fucking playground." She and Nikki got along quite well, and for the first time since Hally, she felt that she had a close friend that was her physical equal. She missed this feeling because normal girls were resentful and envious. Leah and Nikki's long-legged strides matched each other when they glided down the street; they created a nice contrast with Leah's blond hair that was lightened even more due to the advice of a stylist, and Nikki's dark brown hair that was almost black.

She loved that Nikki wasn't jealous because her career seemed to be moving more quickly than hers did when she started. After only a few weeks of being in the city, Leah did a photo spread in *Seventeen*, modeling the new fall trends. The photographer told her she was a natural. When the issue hit the stands, her mother called to tell her that people in Blue Bud were "freaking out" by seeing her in the magazine. Word spread quickly that she was modeling in New York, and lots of people were curious about her career and life. Leah was half-asleep during this conversation, recovering from a night of celebrating the photo spread with Nikki, and her boyfriend Reid. Her head pounded and her nose was completely congested. But she was thrilled. It was gratifying to prove to her step-dad that she could make it. He was opposed to her going to New York and postponing college. She accepted his criticism in silence, and wondered why he overestimated the value of his opinions. When he grew frustrated with her indifference, an ugly aggression arose. He said he'd give her one year off before he'd still pay her college tuition, and he wouldn't help pay for anything in New York because he knew what happened to young girls in the city. She wanted to ask him if he'd ever been to New York, but that would sound too much like arguing.

When Leah got off the phone with her mother, she thought about how she might be the most well known person in Blue Bud history. She could think of no one else who had suffered what she went through at fourteen, only to be discovered by a modeling agent at seventeen. She considered herself part of a rare minority of individuals to be plucked out of obscurity with no precedent. A sense of opportunity to do something with her extraordinary life manifested in an idea: she would try to get her journal published as a book one day. I'm going to be traveling the world, and the public is always interested in models, she thought. And how many people can you think of with fathers who've raped and murdered their best friend? Rape and murder... the absurdity of the awfulness had to mean something. It would be called, *The Notorious Leah S.,* because that's exactly how she felt... notorious.

Nikki and Leah happened to be working in Paris together when Nikki turned twenty-three. "Promise me you won't tell anyone about my birthday," she said to Leah as they sauntered in heels towards a party that some photographer was hosting.

"What's the big deal about your birthday?"

"I don't know...birthdays are depressing. You're only nineteen—you still have time."

"Twenty-three's young."

Nikki shrugged. "You'll see."

The party was typical fashion week fare; the apartment was massive, with tall ceilings and chandeliers, the lights were dim while dance music blasted through a stereo; beautiful women walked around knowing they belonged. People sat together in small groups and talked as they sipped wine. They recognized a model they knew named Estrelle, who had the "twenty minute habit," meaning every twenty minutes she'd disappear into a bathroom for a few minutes. They watched Estrelle enter a bedroom with two other girls, which indicated to them where people disappeared into for more illicit activity.

141

This prompted Leah to whisper in Nikki's ear, "Did you get the stuff?"

Nikki had a regular guy who made deliveries to her hotel. He was a former photographer's assistant who was accustomed to procuring blow for photographers and models. "My bullet's full," she replied with a grin. "He gave me a deal because of my birthday."

"That's awesome. Shall we?"

They poured glasses of white wine for themselves and went into the bedroom, where they were greeted by Estrelle. There were friendly hellos from people throughout the room, most of whom knew Nikki. Estrelle reclined on the king-sized bed barefoot, dressed in a silky plum colored slip dress. Her black hair and black eyes gleamed in the candlelight. Leah admired her dark, exotic look. In person, she was just as stunning as she was in her print ads.

Estrelle hunched over a mirror and did a line of coke with a rolled up dollar bill.

"Here you go," Estrelle said, pushing the mirror towards Leah and Nikki. "Compliments of Michel." She pointed with her chin to the other side of the room, where a small man in plaid pants and a white t-shirt raised his glass. He appeared indifferent to a girl, looking no older than sixteen, who had her arms draped around his slight frame.

Nikki did a line and said, "I take it she's the wannabe for the night."

"You know it," said Estrelle. Leah's quizzical look made Estrelle add, "A wannabe model."

"Oh."

Michel was often sought after by models, or girls who wanted to be models because of his impressive magazine work. There was a rumor that when Estrelle first arrived in Paris, she showed up unannounced at his flat every day with her book until he answered the door. They ended up being lovers, which led to him shooting her for some high profile magazine ads. Their relationship then segued into a mischievous friendship.

There were many fascinating rumors about Estrelle. Some said she was the daughter of a big Columbia drug dealer, compelling her to model in order to escape the violence of her homeland. There was another rumor that she was the mistress of a famous French filmmaker when she was only seventeen.

Leah did a line and looked at the wannabe. She was very pretty, but not quite right for the modeling world. She was a strawberry blond who was blessed with a fair, creamy complexion. But her legs were too thick, and she was perhaps two inches too short to model, although it was hard to tell when she stood next to Michel, who resembled a young Roman Polanski.

"Who did you walk for today, Leah?" asked Estrelle.

"Balenciaga and Chloe."

"Very cool. So, what do you think of your first Paris fashion week? I hope Nikki has been showing you the ropes?"

"Overall, it's a lot harder than I thought it would be. It can be hectic changing so quickly. And yes, Nikki has been a tremendous help."

"She's a natural," Nikki interjected.

Estrelle tilted her head to the side with a slight smile. She said to Leah, "You seem different from the other new girls... more honest. Where are you from?"

"Illinois. We've mastered sincerity in the Midwest. If you can fake that, you've got it made." Both Estrelle and Nikki cracked up laughing. Even though Leah was younger, she felt older because she could quote people like George Burns, Woody Allen, or Groucho Marx, and fool people into thinking it was her wit, and not theirs. She had her father to thank for this, for exposing her to old Jewish comedians when she was a kid.

"You'll have to tell me all about your Indiana sometime," said Estrelle. "Excuse me a moment." She went over to Michel and whispered something in his ear.

Nikki and Leah became aware of the attention of some leering guy, so they went into Michel's bathroom together and locked the door. Nikki unscrewed her bullet, which resembled a silver tube of lipstick, and poured some coke from it onto the back of the toilet. She then chopped it with a razor blade that she kept in an Altoids tin. Leah took this as her cue to roll up a dollar bill.

"Estrelle's something else, isn't she?" said Nikki.

"She's crazy gorgeous."

"I know."

"Where is she from?"

"Costa Rica, I think. Or maybe Columbia." She did a line. "I'll let you in on a secret. She and Michel like to play a game at parties—

143

they pick out a girl and try to get her to do something she normally doesn't do. Usually it's the wannabe. I have a feeling that's what they're discussing right now."

"*Les Liasons dangereuses.*"

"Huh? Oh yeah, I liked that movie."

"Is it usually sexual stuff?"

Nikki smiled. "Yeah, and sometimes it's interesting to watch. Michel's actually rich, you know. He comes from old money and doesn't even have to work—he just wants to because otherwise he'll get bored. His family owns a home in Venice, and every year he hosts a masked ball. One year, he lured a young girl into his bedroom—she had stars in her eyes because of his money, and because he's kinda sexy, you know. I remember she had on this beautiful, full velvety ball gown. He made her lie down on his bed, with a mask on that covered her eyes. He pulled her panties off and said, 'Remember what you promised... I get to do what I want for ten minutes.' Then, without her knowing, Estrelle crawls out from under the bed and totally goes down on her."

Leah's eyes widened in shock as she pictured the scene. "How do you know this?"

"I was in the room watching behind a dressing screen. I was in there anyway with Reid, and Michel said I should stay for a surprise. I had no idea what they were gonna do. They're so naughty!"

"What did the girl do when she found out it was Estrelle?"

"Ha! She climaxed so hard that she didn't care. She ended up sucking Michel off while Estrelle touched her."

"That's pretty wild." Leah began to feel aroused.

When they stepped out of the bathroom, they were surprised to see the bedroom cleared out, except for Estrelle, Michel, and the young girl. The girl looked surprised to see Nikki and Leah. Michel said to her, "Don't worry, they're with us. Have a seat, Girls." Nikki looked at Leah and shrugged as they sat down on a divan. Estrelle and the girl sat on the bed and began kissing. "Okay, Ladies. Let's see," said Michel. Estrelle slipped the straps of her dress off her shoulders and lowered her dress to reveal her full, plump breasts. She did the same with the girl's dress, and began lightly caressing her nipples. Michel touched himself, while Nikki did another line. Leah felt a burning desire between her legs, but suppressed the feeling by looking away.

November 17
"Exhibitionist in Training"
One thing I learned in Paris is that being a model=entrée. Nikki and I don't wait in lines at clubs, and we're invited to parties every night. It's all arbitrary and stupid, in a way. The genetic determination of height and metabolism, mixed with symmetrical features makes me an international citizen of the world. Guess I won the genetic lottery.

Listen to me going on about myself. This is my point about models being exhibitionists. In order to be one, you have to have a sense of yourself as an object. And in most cases, a sex object. I think a lot of models are so used to being objectified, that they get turned on by turning other people on.

Nikki definitely knows a lot about what people do in this business. She told me about this famous photographer who gets girls to do things by promising them photo shoots, which may or may not happen. I wonder what sort of kinky stuff Nikki's done. She doesn't say much about herself. Everyone edits her life story, except for me.

The full surreal aspect of a model's life didn't hit Leah until she went to Tokyo. She flew there alone for a jewelry ad, which was intimidating, but since other models flew all over the world, she told herself to get used to it. She was grateful for the downers Nikki gave her, which made the thirteen-hour flight bearable.

She found the crowds and streets of Tokyo unbelievably strange and exciting. It felt odd being a minority the first time—a blond in a sea of black-haired people. As she walked around, she was struck by the esoteric way that a lot of young people dressed. She looked at a pair of teenaged girls who wore many layers of multi-colored and multi-textured clothing, with seven-inched platform boots. At first, she found this look interesting and creative. But when she saw so many others dressed equally as odd, the effect faded, and she decided they were trying too hard. She made a mental note to buy a camera and begin a photo log to supplement her book.

The photo shoot was with another model, Daria, a stunning woman who was half-Japanese and half-Canadian. She told Leah that it was ironic that this was her first time in Japan, despite her heritage; she was a full-fledged Canadian, born and raised in Toronto. Her flat

145

accent and friendly manner struck Leah as being distinctly "Midwestern," which she found funny—she flew halfway around the world to work with a girl whose friendly demeanor felt close to home.

For the shoot, Leah and Daria wore silver evening gowns and posed with diamond jewelry. After the shoot, Leah looked in the mirror said, "I wish I could keep this dress." She admired its fabric and cut.

"Maybe we can." In perfect sounding Japanese, Daria spoke to the photographer. After he responded, she said to Leah, "Today's our lucky day. He said we could keep them."

"Wow, I didn't know you could just come out and ask that."

"I hear a lot of actors and models take stuff at photo shoots all the time without asking."

Leah was impressed that Daria could switch between languages, and speak English with no accent. "It must be fascinating to be here and speak Japanese."

Daria beamed with happiness. "It's amazing. Toronto has a small Japanese community, and I spoke it with my mom, but here...I've been talking like crazy to everyone. I asked someone for directions even though I wasn't lost. I wonder if he thought, 'That half breed sure has a funny Canadian accent!'" They both laughed at the joke. In an exaggerated "Canadian voice" she continued, "Oh yeah, this sushi here sure is good, eh?" Leah found her hilarious. It was refreshing to meet another model who wasn't vacuous, and actually cracked jokes. "So, do you want to go back to my hotel room?"

January 20
"Why Not?"

When I first met Daria, I was struck by her exotic beauty. Then I found out she was super bright—she was discovered by a scout in London while taking classes at Cambridge. [Note to self: Go back to school eventually!] This made me wonder if people with larger gene pools are naturally more intelligent. (She's Eurasian.) Frankly, I've always wondered this about myself. Nobody knows I'm Jewish and Scandinavian—a stark contrast. Perhaps having more information on the genetic code is inherently good. My mom was stupidly ashamed of my dad's Jewishness. When I was around ten or eleven, she told me that I didn't have to tell anyone I was half Jewish because she didn't think "Gold" was Jewish-sounding, and because I'm so blond and blue-eyed. What a freak. (More on her later.)

Daria was the one who propositioned me. When we went back to her hotel, she started casually touching me, like a hand on my arm or thigh during conversation, as if we were old friends. Then she came out and asked, "Have you ever been with a woman before?" When I said no, she told me that she hadn't either until recently, and it was the best thing she'd ever done, sexually speaking. She said it always makes her climax, and that I'd probably love it. We started kissing and I let her go down on me. Why not? I closed my eyes and could barely believe what was happening. I felt like she understood everything I was feeling, because it wasn't long ago that it was her first time. The weird thing is, ever since Paris I've been thinking about this sort of stuff… fooling around with a woman. It's only natural. Afterwards, she said, "I'll bet that was better than any boyfriend of yours." I told her that I'd never been with a man. This was my first sexual experience, which I think shocked and flattered her. For some reason, we both found this really funny. In my opinion, this is just one more thing that makes my life unique. I had a great time in Tokyo.

At age twenty, Leah was offered her first cover—for British *ELLE*. As soon as she got the good news, she ran into the living room to tell Nikki, and for the first time, Nikki wasn't excited for her. The moment clarified that Leah would move ahead in her career while she would not—she'd never been asked to do a cover, and she never would be. Making matters worse, Nikki just heard from a friend that she didn't get a Ralph Lauren ad she wanted badly because they thought she was "too ordinary". The recent disappointments at go sees were starting to get to her. She wondered if it would help to get Botox injections in her forehead.

Nikki was happy that at least things were going well between her and Reid. She always pictured herself marrying a high-powered lawyer, businessman, doctor, or a trust fund type. But Reid did well as a nightclub owner. It wasn't the most stable business, but the money was great. She wondered why Leah never dated men, even though guys hit on her constantly. Some of them were handsome and successful, and she treated them all like shit. She heard a rumor that Leah made out with a girl at a party, but she didn't want to ask and be nosy.

As usual, Anna called too early in the morning. She wanted to congratulate Leah when the issue of *ELLE* hit the stands. "You looked so beautiful on that cover. You're like a celebrity here!" said Anna.

"Thanks, Mom."

"Are they gonna put you on any American magazine covers?

"I don't know."

"A writer from the *Blue Bud American* called yesterday. They want to know if you'd do an interview with them through email."

"I don't know...I'll have to think about it." She was flattered that people back home were interested in her. But her instinct told her that it was "uncool" to cater to the people she rose above. It's always more interesting to be aloof. This made her think of her step-dad, and what he must think of her career. "How's Danny?"

"Oh, he's fine. We started golfing. We're probably gonna join the country club."

"You better not tell them we're Jewish."

"Leah! That's not funny—"

"Mom, I'm just kidding. So, I guess I don't need Danny to pay that college tuition."

"Now, Leah...we're both proud that you're doing so well, but college isn't a bad idea. Especially since you're so smart. I'm sure Northwestern will still let you in. Don't they have your acceptance on file somewhere?"

Leah didn't know how to respond, so she just laughed. She found it hilarious that her mother would have an opinion about college since she never went herself, nor did she ever hold a job. Leah made more money modeling in one year than her mom made in her whole life.

Leah moved out when it became apparent that Nikki wanted to spend more time alone with Reid. It was time to move on; their friendship grew strained as Nikki struggled to get booked for modeling jobs and began to focus more attention on Reid. Plus, she began questioning Leah's cocaine use. One night she made a caustic remark about Leah doing coke at a friend's apartment on a Tuesday night. "Who orders cocaine so early in the week on a Tuesday?" she said, before asking for a bump. (Weeks earlier, Nikki called her dealer for a blow delivery on a Wednesday.) Leah didn't dignify this with a response because she felt sorry for Nikki.

Their parting was amicable, but Leah was deeply disappointed. Nikki had been a good friend, but as time passed, she began to see her as common: Nikki was a beautiful girl who never challenged her mind since she'd been told her entire life that she was pretty. She liked to talk about herself while expressing no interest in others. Leah was relieved to no longer be subjected to her degenerate rap music.

December 2

The Agony and the Absurdity

Mom called to see if I was coming home for Christmas. I haven't been home in two years because of work, so I probably should. But I don't want to. It would be annoying to run into people from high school and be bombarded with questions. I'd love it if Mom stayed with me, especially since I have my awesome new apartment, but then she'd have to bring Danny. Yuck.

She brought up some unpleasant business about Dad. She's been feeling guilty about never visiting him in prison. Neither of us has ever visited him. It's been six years now. She actually started crying on the phone, which freaked me out. Maybe she misses certain things about him that she doesn't get from Danny. Or maybe she gets like this around Christmas because of all the family memories. Sometimes I miss him too, and then I think of Hally. I told Mom to go to the mantle above the fireplace and look at the photo of Hally and me at our junior high graduation dance. I told her that any time she feels guilty, she should look at that photo and remind herself that that was the night Dad killed her. Saying this only made her cry harder. Oops. What do you say in a situation like this? It's absurd.

The conversation with her mom left Leah shaken— much too stressed for a Saturday night. She was on her way to a party in the Meatpacking District when thoughts of her father conjured man-hating emotions. Usually, she suppressed these feelings because she associated bigoted thinking with her mom, whom she considered uneducated and child-like.

She knew that it wouldn't take expensive sessions of therapy to figure out that her anger towards her dad affected her own sexuality. She'd never been with a man, although she'd had flings with three different women. Despite this, she didn't consider herself a lesbian. She knew that she'd eventually have sex with a man, but something about it disturbed her. It was difficult to articulate the fear and anger she related to sex with men. Sometimes she forced herself to clarify these feelings in her mind. It usually distilled to this: being penetrated by a man meant having no control.

Leah chatted with a group of girlfriends at the party when Estrelle tapped her on the shoulder. "Hello there, Princess Leah." They hugged and kissed the air as their cheeks lightly touched.

"Hey, Estrelle. Good to see you! I saw your Pantene commercial. You looked amazing!"

"Thank you so much! How are you?"

"Great—I just moved into my own apartment."

"Very cool." She leaned in closer and said, "I heard about you and Nikki. Do you want to step into the bedroom for a moment? I want to chat with you."

"Sure."

They went into a large bedroom that had gray concrete floor, black and white nude photos of women on the walls, and huge metal candelabra on either side of a brass bed. Leah thought that the room's starkness and metal lent a sadomasochistic vibe. Her suspicions were confirmed when she noticed silk braided bondage cords at the corners of the bed. Some people are so fucked up, she thought.

"He's got this cool private room back here," said Estrelle.

The "room" was actually a walk-in closet filled with clothes and various fetish costumes, and it was large enough to have a little couch and a thin sliver of a coffee table. Estrelle shut the door and pulled a small plastic baggie from her purse. "Want a little bump?" she asked.

"Yeah."

Estrelle scooped a bit of coke with a pen cap into each nostril and handed the baggie to Leah. "I wanted to talk to you about Nikki," said Estrelle. "She was talking shit about you the other night over at my friend's apartment. I wasn't sure if you knew this."

"What was she saying?"

"She said that you think you're smarter than everyone else, you flirt with Reid, and she said something about you doing a live sex show with another girl at a party once."

"She's ridiculous. I don't flirt with Reid. We talk about books sometimes because Nikki only reads magazines. And I did not do a live sex show. But I know what she's talking about." She did another bump and continued, "I'll be honest with you… last summer, I was with my friend, Michelle, and three other guys on a yacht in the Hamptons. The guy who owned the yacht is some bigwig over at Sony. We were all fucked up on blow, champagne, and pot. It was crazy. He said that he'd give Michelle and I a thousand dollars each in cash if they could watch us make out."

"Interesting." Estrelle wriggled in her seat from excitement.

"We've made out before, but never in front of anyone. So the first thought that entered my mind was that we'd be getting paid to do what we do anyway. There was a friendly vibe on the boat, and I don't know… I just thought it would be funny. Maybe I made a mistake. But I don't think I did anything wrong, per se. Nothing that warrants being ridiculed behind my back by Nikki. It was like a joke."

"I agree with you. She's a hypocrite. I don't think she's really your friend, and I wanted you to know this because you've always seemed like a nice person. You're not like all those other girls who talk shit all the time."

Leah began to cry. It was the suddenness that caught her off guard; Nikki got on her nerves at times, but they were also friends who helped each other. (She recently offered to help Nikki study for the SAT since her own scores were so high.) This wasn't the only thing that made her cry. There were too many emotions to handle at the moment. The thoughts bounced around in her head at lightning speed—about Nikki, her mom, her dad. She began to hyperventilate. Her heart raced and she sweated profusely. It had been years since she'd had a full-blown panic attack.

"Are you okay, Sweetie?" Estrelle placed her arm on Leah's shoulder. "Were you doing a lot of blow earlier?"

Leah shook her head. "It's not the coke. I need to—" Before finishing her thought, she lay down on the rug, closed her eyes, and breathed deeply as tears streamed down her cheeks. "Don't worry… sometimes I get panic attacks."

"I'm sorry. I hope I didn't upset you." Estrelle was worried this was all her fault.

"It wasn't you at all. It's…" She curled up in the fetal position and cried while covering her face.

"What's wrong? You can talk to me."

Leah had never told anyone in New York about her father. She kept it all to herself and allocated her feelings to her journal. Her instinct was to remain silent about it, but something about Estrelle made it seem okay to talk.

She sat up and wiped her tears with a tissue that Estrelle handed her. She then proceeded to tell her the entire story about Hally, her dad, how he's on death row, and how she and her mom never visit or write to him. It all made Estrelle cry too, especially when Leah told her that her dad might be executed at any time; whenever her mom called, she thought it might be The Call, informing her that her father's time was near.

Later that night, Leah was surprised by her own outpouring. It was a terrible thing to always suppress the emotion that shaped her self-identity. She discovered that crying in front of Estrelle made her feel ashamed, and she didn't know why. She was lying in bed thinking hard about why she associated crying with weakness, especially since Estrelle was sympathetic. There was something distinctly unfeminine, she thought, about her distain for sharing her emotions.

A glimmer of insight occurred when she closed her eyes and let her mind travel back to when she was fourteen. It was after Hally's funeral, on the ride home with her mom. Leah felt numb while silently staring out the car window at houses, streets, and fields Hally would never see again. Anna had been quiet all day, which was out of character for her. The silence must have bothered her, because she felt the need to turn on the car radio and find a station. The volume was up too high as the radio crackled and skipped from one station to the next. When it came to a Led Zeppelin song, Anna remarked, "Yuck. Your father loves this band. At least I won't have to listen to this crap anymore."

At this precise moment, Leah told herself that expressing pain and anger was meaningless. It didn't change anything because no one understood. Her mom didn't understand—she seemed almost happy on a certain level to be free of her husband.

December 15
Who is Matthew Gold?

I overhear a lot of people say that their parents were good or bad, or responsible for their depression or whatever. There's a lot of blame out there when it comes to parents. The ironic thing is, overall my dad was pretty good. I have early memories of him spending lots of time with me, teaching me to read and count, teaching me basic math concepts, years before anyone else my age was learning these things. When I entered kindergarten, I felt like I was surrounded by retarded people. That's why I was able to skip the first grade.

I don't know exactly why, but when I got a little older, I was no longer "daddy's little girl." There was something about him that I didn't like, which made me not care what he thought, as if I were better than him. (I often don't care what others think.) There was something about his slouching, downtrodden demeanor that bothered me. In retrospect, it's obvious that my mom had something to do with this. She complained and henpecked him all the time, and he never stood up for himself. Maybe I would have respected him more if he did. So I mistreated my own dad by being cold to him. Normally this would make a person feel bad and apologize, but now I wonder if I was reacting to something beyond my mother's influence. Maybe on a subconscious level I knew that he was seriously messed up.

It's obvious that he was sick. It takes a lot to rape and murder a fourteen year old girl, no less one who happens to be your daughter's best friend. Rape and murder, rape and murder. The phrase echoes in my head because it's part of my life: my dad raped and murdered Hally. None of the psychiatrists could confirm insanity, which would have changed his sentence. Does this mean he isn't insane? I choose to believe that he is, and the doctors are wrong. So does this mean he shouldn't die? Not a day goes by that I don't wonder this.

The thing that disturbs me most is the fact that he was sick, but savvy enough to hide it. It doesn't make sense. Nothing about my dad makes sense, and there's nothing I can do about it. All I know is that he's proven that no matter what, you never know what dark, chaotic forces lie beneath the surface, or what could trigger violence. Nothing in this world will ever surprise me.

Leah felt giddy in Estrelle's presence, as if she were with an older, wiser sister she could emulate. Over time, Leah's intimidation faded, and things between them started to change. Whenever Leah visited Estrelle's sparsely elegant Tribeca loft, she felt completely content, with a consciousness existing both in the present and future; she appreciated where she was, and knew she'd look back on this time as being important, just as important as being discovered at the Chicago Water Tower. Despite this, Leah didn't refer to Estrelle as a "girlfriend" in her journal, even though they were in a sexual relationship. She didn't think everything had to have a label. She wrote in her journal, "I'm beyond labels."

Her bond with Estrelle was characterized by disclosure, starting with the time she cried in front of her in that strange little room. Since then, their frank discussions often occurred after sex; their life stories were shared with no regard for editing. Estrelle was molested by her cousin when she was nine, and he was twelve. She said it was difficult to be angry considering they were both kids when it happened. "It was more like curiosity," she explained, "although sometimes I felt forced." Her cousin would take off her panties and explore her body with his fingers. Leah was appalled, and surprised that Estrelle wasn't angry—it only confirmed to her that males were out to gratify themselves no matter what. The intensity of this response led to conversation about her obvious anger towards men. She admitted that the idea of being penetrated by a man made her feel sick, like she would be taken advantage of. It was a flawed line of thinking, and she hated to be dogmatic, but she didn't care because she was content to be where she was now—with a woman she respected and admired.

Leah also revealed that she liked to tease and punish men by letting them watch her make out with another woman. She discovered this while on that boat in the Hamptons. "I've been meaning to ask you about that," said Estrelle. "I find that very enticing." She gently circled Leah's breast with her fingertip and ran it down her side. "Would you like to do that again? We could bring some poor sap over here. It might be fun."

Leah never thought she'd be in a long-term relationship with a woman. In an old journal entry, she wrote that "Estrelle's impulsiveness was exhilarating because she made it seem like nothing was every truly wrong." They understood each other because their unusual lives removed the normal constraints of rules. Estrelle's father was a government official in Columbia who was educated in

Switzerland. When Estrelle became a target for kidnapping, she left for Paris, to live with her dad's best friend from school, a filmmaker who promised to look after her education. There, she got into modeling and has been on her own since she was seventeen.

Eventually Leah admitted to herself that it wasn't all just fun experimentation, this relationship with Estrelle. It felt strange yet liberating to admit this in her journal, which for her meant that it would be read by others someday. This wasn't the most comfortable concept, but she felt that her integrity as a diarist meant being completely honest.

It was all there in the journal: the cocaine, the wild parties where orgy-like situations arose (usually when overseas) because they were surrounded by people who used sex and power to transcend boredom. She wrote about her modeling gigs, and the strange nights when Estrelle and Leah would go out to clubs and parties and prey upon some young, nerdy, college type of boy to bring back to Estrelle's loft. (They liked the ones that didn't realize how handsome they were.) After making sure the guy was harmless, they'd demonstrate on each other the best way to please a woman.

As her father's impending execution grew nearer, Leah worked harder and harder on her book, perhaps to distract herself, or maybe because there was an urgent sense that the book would end with his death. She thought it made narrative sense.

April 13
"The End Is Near"
I don't know what I'd do without Estrelle because everything around me is falling apart. My mom is freaking out, calling me almost every day, just to talk about stuff. I feel bad for her because I think she's bored and not as happy with Danny as she thought she'd be. She can be very transparent. It's obvious that she wants to discuss the banal minutia of her life so that she doesn't have to think about dad's execution. It's been ten years and we've both never visited or written him. It sounds more unbelievable on paper than it feels. Time goes by quickly, and let's face it—his crime made it seem like he forfeited his humanity.

I used to have nightmares that he'd try to kill me. Now I have nightmares about Mom and I going to Hell— a place I don't necessarily believe in. If there is a god, I wonder if we'll look morally worse than him. I know he feels terrible regret. For all I know, he could be a re-born again Jew for Jesus, if such a thing exists. Maybe Mom and I will end up in the same circle of Hell as absentee dads—people who made the conscious decision to disengage from their own flesh and blood.

They were having brunch at a café when Leah got the call on her cell phone from her mom. "It's time to come home," said Anna.

"When?"

"Two days."

When Leah hung up, Estrelle took her hand and said, "I'll be there for you, if you want."

During the plane ride home, Leah glibly wrote in her journal, "I'm now flying home with my lesbian lover to attend my father's execution." Anna didn't know about Estrelle, or anything else about her personal life for that matter. Leah saw no reason to "come out" during this visit, which Estrelle understood.

When they arrived at Leah's home, Anna greeted them at the door, and made Estrelle feel welcome. Danny gave Leah a hug, and seemed genuinely glad to see her. It felt strange to be in the home where she lived for less than four years before leaving. It was a reminder that her true roots in Blue Bud had been uplifted and removed. Leah noticed that the house looked mainly the same, but there were more little embellishments—porcelain Lladro figurines displayed in a tall glass case, framed watercolor paintings from various countries, and other little knick knacks from their travels. Leah imagined her mom trying to impress dinner guests with her "conversation pieces."

Danny seemed nervous as he stupidly asked Estrelle in a loud and overly annunciated voice if he could get her anything to drink; her dark features spelled "foreign" in his mind. Anna was annoyed, but accustomed to her husband's gaffes as she busied herself in the kitchen with a strained expression. Anna was fifty now, and still strikingly beautiful. Leah felt a rush of love towards her mother, despite her deep criticisms. Leah still saw her mother as a child who never learned independence. And now she seemed trapped—it was by her own doing, but she was trapped nonetheless.

Matthew was to be executed in a little town called Linwood, which was a short drive from Blue Bud. The girls took a separate car to the prison because Leah found Danny physically repulsive. His presence irked her, not only because he'd gained nearly thirty pounds and was overly polite to her in a cloying way, but because he exuded nervous energy that made everything more difficult than it already was.

When they got to the prison, Danny and Estrelle went to a waiting area, while Leah and Anna were brought into the witness room. There was a window facing the execution chamber that was covered with a black curtain.

Hally's parents, Mr. and Mrs. Rice, were there when they arrived. Leah was struck by how old they looked, despite them being around the same age as her mom. She barely recognized the couple that used to take her and Hally on camping trips, and pray together before eating dinner. Their faces were withered, and they seemed smaller, as if extreme grief had the ability to shrink a person. They were a quiet, humble couple who went to the Baptist church every Sunday. Hally used to talk about how hypocritical her dad was for going to church, but falling asleep half the time because he was hungover. But she loved her parents. She never judged them the way Leah judged her father—she wasn't capable of ugly behavior.

As Leah gave the Rices a tearful hug, she was reminded of conversations she had with Hally about church; they both hated being forced to go by their parents because they thought it was boring and unnecessary. Oddly, Leah was now grateful that Hally's parents were Christian. They forgave Matthew, and were able to not hate her and her mom. She and Anna didn't kill Hally, but it was impossible to not feel guilt when she looked into Mr. and Mrs. Rice's red, watery eyes. Matthew once told her that some Jews felt guilty for surviving the Shoah, because they wondered why they were alive while so many others died.

The four of them sat silently in the room that buzzed with bright fluorescent light. They all knew what to expect from lethal injection, yet when the black curtain was pulled to the side, it was shocking to see Matthew Gold strapped down on a gurney, prepared to be injected. Anna made a guttural crying noise when she saw him.

Leah had tried to prepare herself for the sight, but it still seemed unreal, as if executions were too barbaric to actually happen, as if no one deserved them. She saw her father look at the window for a moment and then turn away as tears fell steadily down his cheeks. She knew that he couldn't see through the one-way window. But if he could, would he have looked away? Leah held her mother's hand and also cried, but she suppressed making a sound out of respect for Hally's parents. The Rices suffered a much greater loss, and deserved their closure without distraction.

Matthew was asked if he wanted to make a final statement. After a brief pause, he replied, "No." Leah was confused. After years of never speaking to him, she wondered why he had nothing to say. Why would he have nothing to say after what he did? When the injections began, she wanted to run to the window and pound on it while yelling, "Stop! Let him say something!" But they did let him, and he declined. His resolute tone sounded like his mind was made up to exit the world in silence—to disappear without leaving a mark.

They all watched Matthew die as three injections were administered. Leah took shallow breaths and sat silently as she thought of the time when he taught her to ride a bicycle. He ran alongside her down the street with his hand steadying the back of the seat, until letting go.

There were hugs and tears as everyone met in the prison parking lot and got into their separate cars. Leah couldn't leave her mom and Danny soon enough. Her head was spinning and she felt slightly nauseated.

Leah was too distraught to drive, so she asked Estrelle to drive around on some country roads, not sure where they were going. They rolled the windows down, embracing the silence, with the exception of crickets and wind. The air was crisp, and smelled lush with the onset of spring. They drove past expanses of farmland and little houses, back dropped against a starry sky. It was the landscape of her youth, and of the good life her parents tried to have together. Was the starkness of the environment conducive to inner complication? Would her dad's sickness have been offset by a more satisfying home?

When they made their way back to the main road in Linwood, they realized they were hungry. The only place open was Hardees, so they pulled into the parking lot. Before exiting the car, Leah said,

"Wait a second."

Estrelle's eyes were wet and bloodshot—it took great effort for her to not cry—she didn't want to make things even more difficult for Leah. In a quiet voice, Estrelle asked, "Are you going to be okay?"

Leah slowly shook her head. With her eyes set forward, she spoke in a monotone, "They asked him to make a final statement, and he said nothing. This is my punishment."

"Leah, Sweetie... I don't understand."

"I could have visited or written him, but I chose to remain angry... all these years. It's possible that he hated us." Her brow wrinkled. "I'm not even sure why I'm here. In a sick way, I thought all my pain and anger made me better and more interesting than others...notorious."

Estrelle gently squeezed Leah's hand and handed her a tissue. "You're a good person. You're going to get through this. I'll help you with anything you want." Leah hugged Estrelle, thankful that she was not alone. When she returned to New York, she planned to pursue acting through Estrelle's agent since the modeling assignments were dwindling. She also planned to get her book published.

Having goals distracted the darkness inside from enveloping her. If she didn't have her looks, or Estrelle, there would always be something else extraordinary in her life. Things would go back to normal; reality shifted and transformed like an organic substance. Estrelle and Michel no longer played their games. Soon, Anna would leave Danny and move to New York to be with her daughter.

An emptiness would always exist in Leah's mind—an understanding that deliverance wasn't possible. It was too late.

Leah managed a slight smile before asking, "Was it awful waiting with Danny?"

Estrelle shrugged. "I might as well warn you now—he really thinks you should go to college." They both laughed as they got out of the car and walked through the parking lot.

"Hold on," said Leah, taking her camera out of her purse. "Stand there, so I can get the sign in." She snapped a photo of Estrelle, looking relaxed and solemn, with the glowing orange sign of Hardees behind her. "For my book."